BEYOND DENIAL

Beyond Denial

By

Juri Vancans

2018

United States Copyright Office
Manuscript Registration Number: TXu 1-971-257
Effective Date of Registration:
June 02, 2015

Cover Design: Keli Maffei

ISBN 9781985377424

Other works by Juri Vancans: The Bushido Element

www.jurivancans.com

DEDICATION

To the vanished and extinguished

To the millions

Their names, their works, their loves

Their hopes, their dreams

Their youth, their ages

Their inimitable joys

Their individual heartbreaks

Their lives

All that would have been

Distinctively and exclusively theirs

Eradicated

Taken forever

By a ravenous

Inconceivable

Hate of a people

And a policy of their extermination.

Prologue

Berlin: Fall 1944

SS officers Hans Kroner and Martin Ulricht paced nervously in the grim hallway. They were apprehensive and on the edge of panic. Reichsfuhrer Heinrich Himmler had summoned them to the Berlin Reich Security Office at Prinz-Albrecht-Strasse No.8. The former art museum was now used by the SS and the Gestapo to interrogate, torture, and murder enemies of the Reich. Kroner and Ulricht had been in Poland and Lithuania, liaising between the SS Einsatzgruppen battalions that were exhuming corpses of Jews from massive execution pits and burning the remains.

They had been roused in the middle of the night and ordered back. Fear gripped them because when Himmler directed you to appear before him, it was usually not pleasant—often, it was deadly. Kroner and Ulricht had reviewed any possible mistakes they could have made.

A heavy door opened and an SS guard led them to Himmler.

The Reichsfuhrer stood up and came around his desk. He had a petite gait to his walk, like a held-back little skip. Over dinner just the other night in Poland, several officers had joked about Himmler's sometimes-funny "elfin" walk. Kroner and Ulricht had laughed along with everyone else. Had one of Himmler's SS cronies snitched on them for deriding the Reichsfuhrer's stride?

Himmler didn't look angry or upset. He did not have his usual flat appearance; actually, he looked friendly. *Good sign,* Kroner thought.

Himmler slapped his palms together and said, "I have chosen you two to be my gardeners."

Kroner and Ulricht looked at each other quizzically. They did not ask why or inform Himmler that they knew absolutely nothing about gardening.

Himmler said, "The Third Reich is a big garden. It has expanded and grown into other countries. There are a lot of weeds in our garden of Endlosung."

Endlosung, the Final Solution of the Jewish question, Kroner processed silently. *That's a big garden. Is he talking about a garden of concentration camps?*

Himmler continued, "To be clear, in our garden, weeds are records, directives, policies, films, and photographs of the Final Solution. We have been besieged by the German record-keeping madness. The weeds must be pulled and burned. This is our private operation. Just the three of us. Nothing official, nothing written. You will do this very quietly and very quickly. Alle unkraut aus. All the weeds out. Especially the Totenbuchs. They are the headcount books each camp maintains, showing the number of units liquidated every day."

Ulricht asked, "Units? Do you mean Jews?"

Himmler smiled. "Yes, that's what I mean. Units are Jews. One unit equals one Jew. So, it's Units. Units—not Jews."

"Jawhol, Herr Reichsfuhrer," Ulricht snapped. "Units."

"If any camp commandant does not have the Totenbuchs, or does not turn them over, their names are to be reported to me immediately. Also, inspect all the papers at the camps. Anything even remotely related to the Final Solution must be destroyed."

"Some of those camp commandants outrank me," Kroner said. "What if they refuse to hand over the Totenbuchs?"

Himmler handed Kroner a sheet of paper. "I have anticipated that possibility."

It was an official letter from Himmler to all concerned: *By this direct order of the Reichsfuhrer, all written and photographic records that officers Kroner and Ulricht request are to be given to them immediately.*

"I have complete and total trust in you. I have followed your careers, and I know you can execute this highly secret and critical operation.

"After you have collected the records at each camp take them to a secluded area away from the camp and burn them. Do not burn them at the camp. Do not bring them back here to the Ministry. Do not let anyone see you burn them. Use this procedure with every camp. Never tell anyone anything regarding this operation. It's between us three."

Once outside the Ministry, a smiling Ulricht slapped Kroner on the back. "This is a nice little job. I thought he was going to send us to the Russian front."

"Temporarily it's much better than Russia," Kroner said. "However, when we finish and all the weeds are collected and burned, Himmler is going to have us shot. You do understand that, Martin? We will be tortured first and then shot."

"Shot? Why?"

"You see, we are the weeders. We will have seen and touched all the weeds, the evidence of the Final Solution. We will be as contaminated as the weeds. Himmler wants all evidence of the Final Solution destroyed. If Germany loses the war and he is caught, the Allies will try him for crimes against humanity. They will hang him. So, my friend, alle unkraut aus. All the weeds out. That includes you and me."

Chapter 1

Lake George upper New York State: Summer 1978

Ben yanked the gearshift into reverse to avoid the wooden boat whose pilot appeared oblivious of the impending impact.

They didn't crash—only spray and foam—but it was close. As the careening boat sped away, Ben's eyes were drawn to the name inscribed on its transom, partially obscured by the kicked-up wake. He couldn't believe he had seen that name with that distinctive lettering, here on this lake. Had he read it correctly? He tried to read the name again, but the boat was too far away. That name convoked the loathsome, terrifying past, but here it was on Lake George in Upstate New York, not on the Elbe River in Nazi Germany. He was positive he had seen embellished spirals on the first and last letters, the M and the A, spinning little twirls at the beginning and end of each, exactly as they were emblazoned in his memory, precisely as they were on those same letters as they appeared on the transom of the boat he had sailed as a boy.

He had to see the name again, make sure he had read it correctly. Ben pushed the throttle forward and followed the boat. If it was the name he thought he had read, who was the pilot? That's what drove him. A glimpse of the pilot had revealed nothing identifiable. Of course, he had not seen the man's face, only the back of his white-haired head.

When the wooden boat slowed down near the opposite shore, Ben shifted into neutral, grabbed his binoculars, and focused on the letters on the boat's transom, making sure he had read them correctly. He had. There was the name: *MANNY A*. A name as familiar to him as his own. He shifted gears and headed for the *MANNY A*, then abruptly yanked the shift back and stopped. Ben knew it would be unwise, even dangerous, to just pull up to the *MANNY A* and ask the pilot how it got its name, and if he had named it, ask the why and who and how of everything associated with the name. Ben couldn't do that because the name on the transom was linked to one man—Hans Kroner.

SS Colonel Hans Kroner. A name that made Ben's blood run cold. He shuddered at the prospects, at the reawakened loathing of Kroner's name, at the astounding possibility that Kroner might be alive, as his friend Nazi hunter Hannah Zar insisted.

Ben watched the pilot, who had put on a yellow rain slicker, hoping he would glance back so Ben could see his face. But the man's eyes were fixed straight ahead. The only telltale sign that evoked a memory was the man's stance at the wheel of the *MANNY A*, a raised chin looking down upon the vanquished in disgust. That's what Ben remembered about Kroner. He was a cold-blooded, coldhearted, murdering son of a bitch who always looked down on everyone.

Before long, the *MANNY A* turned around and backed up along a dock on the protected, steep east bank of the lake. Through the binoculars, Ben watched as the man in the yellow slicker stepped onto the dock and tied off the *MANNY A*. Then, the man walked up to a storage shed near the dock. Shortly after, he returned to the boat with a red, five-gallon gas can. After refueling, the man zipped and snapped on a canvas mooring cover to seal off the boat from the weather.

Ben studied the man's movements carefully. He only saw the profile of the man's head, now wearing the yellow slicker's hood half-pulled. Ben thought he detected a limp as the man walked down the dock—another possible connection to Kroner, especially after their violent confrontation on Christmas Eve in 1944, when Ben had failed to kill him.

It was 7:00 p.m. Ben would find out more about the man and his boat as soon as it was dark. He turned his own boat out to the middle of the lake. Until that time, he'd go fishing.

Chapter 2

Ben yanked the landing net out of the holder and peered down into the

black waters. After a fifteen-minute struggle, the lake trout had surrendered

and slid alongside. "Give up, fish." Ben saw the fish roll over, saw its girth

and flank, guessed that it was close to thirty pounds. He lowered the net

and slid it under the fish. As he lifted it, the big trout shook its head in one

last, desperate attempt, then flopped and rolled free. Ben plunged the net

down into the water again, got under the heavy fish, and lifted, but the lake

trout's powerful, forked tail dug for traction, paddled, lunged, and pushed

the rim of the net away. It slid off into the lake. Ben hung over the side. He

stretched and reached with the landing net, but the fish shook its head,

snapped the line, and dove. Off the hook. Gone.

"Damn it!" Ben yelled.

In the dim illumination of the cockpit light, off the lake trout's green

and silver flanks, ricocheted a memory.

Ben saw a silver broach on a woman's green, velvet Yom Kippur dress,

and a silver skull and bones on a man's green-gray, wool uniform. Green

and silver—the raiment of the meek, the livery of the powerful. Out of the

blood of World War II leeched a dark feeling, ruthless, uncompromising,

and deadly. There was the lost face of his mother, there was the failure of all failures—the murder he couldn't prevent and failed to render. And fixed in the darkness was the specter of SS Colonel Hans Kroner.

Ben stowed the fishing gear, turned off the running lights, and focused on the Loran LCD screen. When he was at the longitude and latitude coordinates of the stored waypoint, he turned east and cut his speed to two mph. Piecemeal, he started to make out shapes on the dark lakeside. Night's deviance altered the normal shape and color of things. It took a while, but he found the boat.

He cut off his motor and carefully slid into the empty dock south of where it was tied up. He glanced at his watch. It was almost 10:00 p.m.

He made his way through ankle-deep water along the rocky lakeside, using his penlight in quick flashes to find solid footing. The bank dropped off quickly; he had to hold onto trees and protruding roots. In under a minute, he was on the boat. He went to its transom and saw the black, Gothic-style letters, probably carved out of teak or mahogany: the *MANNY A*. Repressed, bitter memories spewed up as he stared. The letters were exactly as he remembered.

Ben snapped open the mooring cover and looked underneath. No fishing gear, no electronic equipment, only a lapstrake Lyman from the '60s, about an eighteen-footer, perfectly restored, with polished, bright work and even the scent of new marine varnish.

To kill the shivers, he trotted up the terraced stone stairway that led to the house up from the dock. His feet squished from his wet socks inside his sneakers, but the shakes were coming from anticipation, not the raw chill.

The house had a light on in one room downstairs. He peered through the window and saw the back of a white-haired man sitting by a writing desk and looking through a photo album. The man had bony shoulders and a long neck. He moved his head slowly, deliberately from page to page, massaging the back of his neck as if it were stiff or in pain. Ben knew it was the same man he had seen in the boat, but he needed to see his face to identify him.

Ben watched him leaf through the album, wanting to detect something familiar, something recognizable. He remembered steel blue eyes and straight, blond hair. This man had white hair combed straight back and a short, neat, chalky beard. The man poured clear liquor into a tumbler and took a sip. Then, he planted his elbows on the table and dropped his head into his hands. After a long moment, he stretched, yawned, glanced around the room, then turned out the desk light and got up. For a split second, Ben saw a bony face with deep, dark eyes illuminated by a dim light descending the stairway. The eyes were searching for something. They landed on Ben. He froze as the face stared in his direction. In the darkness, he imagined the man was a phantom.

Ben slid away from the window and pressed his back against the cedar shingle siding. After a few seconds, he peeked back in. The man walked tentatively, hobbling slightly, to the foot of the stairs, grabbed the railing with one hand and flipping the light on with the other. Ben jerked back around. The light from the window illuminated the top of a Norway spruce a few feet from the house. A few minutes later, the light went off.

Ben walked out to the road. The name on the mailbox was Van Meer. He flipped down the box's access door. Empty.

Chapter 3

The only house Ben had ever broken into had been the last house he had built. He had to jimmy a double hung window to get in so he could get the truck keys he had left inside.

Van Meer's cottage had two doors. He tried the back first. It was locked, and so was the front. With his pocketknife, he cut two slits in the bottom of the window screen so he could slide open the latches and raise it. He slid the blade between the upper and lower sash, opened the lock, and pushed up on the sash. It was tight. He cut the screen out completely and gave the window a hard push. It opened. He crawled inside.

He walked quietly across the room to the writing desk and took out his penlight.

He opened the album and leafed through it. There were color photos of a Christmas, a graduation, a wedding, a child, and a teenager and the man with the beard. He had small eyes, pale skin. His expression was grim, tarnished perhaps, even slightly pathetic—definitely not the pitiless, unfeeling facial cast of SS Colonel Hans Kroner.

Ben closed the album. On the desk were open letters, bills, all addressed to Pieter Van Meer. There were envelopes in the letter cubbies. He took one out. The return address was San Diego. He scanned the words.

Dear Daddy,

-----Mom has been dead five years now-----you shouldn't be alone-----.
Love, Mandy.

Mandy? Probably short for Amanda.

At this moment, Ben thought he should abandon the break-in. Get out
before the man woke up and called the police. The guy was not Hans
Kroner. *Accept it.* But Ben didn't move to leave.

He opened the single drawer in the center of the desk. Pencils, paper
clips, business cards, instruction booklet for an answering machine, and a
small envelope. In the envelope was an old black-and-white photograph of
a two or three-year-old boy-sitting on a lawn with a German shepherd
puppy standing by his side. When Ben turned the photo over and saw
November 14, 1931 written on the back, he froze and held his breath. He
flipped the picture over again and studied it closer, especially the boy's
face, and the striped ball on the grass. He slid the picture in his shirt pocket
and let out his breath.

Ben leafed through the album and found a packet of pictures that had
not been displayed. He found a photograph of the man when his beard was
dark, when he looked vigorous, youthful, smiling through porcelain white
teeth, standing proud on a boat in a turtleneck sweater and a white
captain's cap. August 1964 was the date on the back of that picture. Ben
slid that picture in his shirt pocket, along with a more recent photo where
the man was sitting in a rocking chair by a window, looking out to a snow-
covered frozen lake. The branch of a pine tree weighed down by the snow
hung in front of the window. A pipe was clamped between the man's teeth,

and he was wearing a black turtleneck. In the branches of the reflected pine tree, Ben could make out an almost kaleidoscopic image of the person taking the picture, a wide face cut up by light and shadow and indistinct overlapping reflections.

He opened some of the other drawers, but didn't find anything of interest. The photographs—except for the boy and dog, and the shocking November 14, 1931 date—struck nothing familiar or identifiable. He'd have to mail the pictures to Hannah Zar who would compare them to the photos of Kroner in her organization's records. Quietly, he pushed the chair back and got up.

He stood at the bottom of the stairs and listened to the steady rain on the metal roof. He wanted to go up, then decided against it. He turned to leave, but when he heard what sounded like snoring, he placed his foot on the first step.

The stair treads were covered with a dark carpet runner dotted with small, iron gray crosses. Ben came to the top step and saw that the room the man was sleeping in was right in front of the landing. He stepped up to the doorway. The man snored erratically. The room smelled of pine. The only illumination came from a night-light plugged into an outlet near the floor.

The man slept on his back with his hands across his chest, like someone in a casket. As Ben stepped closer to look at his face, he saw a black pistol on the nightstand. The man's breathing was rough and phlegmy. There was an anguished expression on his face. Possibly the expression was a telltale of the man's character. Of his life as a killer.

Ben glanced at the pistol as he moved closer. It was a large caliber, perhaps a .44 or .45. It wasn't the Luger pistol that Ben had used as a boy. He remembered the weight and feel of that Luger, could still feel its recoil, the smell of the exploding powder and his ultimate failure to use it. Also on the nightstand were a glass of water and a container of pills. Ben picked up the pills. Valium.

He glanced at the man's pallid hands and leaned closer. An unidentified smell sent a ripple of nausea through him.

Instinctively, he reached for the pistol. As his fingers curled around the crackled grip, he froze and stared at an artificial leg propped up against the nightstand.

He tiptoed down to the foot of the bed, still holding the pistol. The blankets were tucked in tightly under the mattress, military-style. Where the right leg should have been, the blanket was flat to about the knee area.

The man stirred and rolled over onto his side. Ben stopped, waited, and aimed the pistol at him. Then, the man was still again, breathing heavily. There was nothing familiar about the sleeping face. Ben had to hear the man speak, see him with his eyes open in the accuracy of daylight. Quickly and quietly, he replaced the pistol on the nightstand, backed away and went down the stairs, lowered and locked the window, and went out the door. He walked around the house and picked up the cut-out screen and took it with him.

Daylight. Ben needed the light of day to see the man's face up close, to hear his voice, to see how he moved, how he stood. Then, he'd know if he had found the supposedly, reportedly deceased SS Colonel Hans Kroner.

Chapter 4

The wind had died; it was cooler, and a fog was descending on the black water. A dim and spectral night lay ahead. Ben wanted to look inside the *MANNY A* one more time. He stepped into the boat, crawled under the mooring cover, and looked around, opening a storage compartment in the helm area and scanning it with his flashlight. There was a small, plastic-covered notebook. He flipped through the pages; all were blank.

Ben glanced around the boat and decided on a plan that would start by siphoning gas from the *MANNY A* into his boat.

Thirty minutes later, he untied his boat, *Drifter*, boarded, pushed off, and paddled out. When he was about 100 yards out, he started the trolling motor and moved out on the lake another 300 yards. Then, he turned off the motor and dropped anchor. The depth finder read thirty feet. Ben glanced around and could see no more than ten feet in any direction. He crawled into the cuddy where he kept a sleeping bag and a change of clothes.

Dry in the sleeping bag, the boat gently swinging on the anchor rode, he fell asleep as the black night enclosed him.

The SS officer pushed the boy into the filthy swimming pool. The boy sank to the bottom, where, suspended above the slimy floor, was a woman in a green dress with her face turned away from him. Just as the woman started to drift toward him, started to turn her face toward him, the boy floated up from the bottom, and again he didn't see her face. When he broke through the surface, the boy gulped a quick mouthful of air and dove in again. The boy swam down to the bottom and looked for the woman. He wanted to see her face if only for a split second. He saw her shape in the murky water for an instant, then she floated out of sight and the boy swam up for more air. The SS man snagged the boy under the armpit with a long, metal hook, pulled him out of the stagnant pool, flopped him down on a concrete slab, and held him down with his shiny, black boot. As the boy lay on the concrete, he saw a looming wall of fire, choking smoke, a girl with immense blue eyes swelled with tears, and an ashen-faced boy with rolled-up sleeves running through a burning city with a dog by his side. Then, someone faceless who could have just witnessed a murder was fleeing through a snowstorm on a motorcycle.

Ben woke up with a start. He was drenched in sweat. He crawled out of the sleeping bag and out to the deck. Had he screamed? There had been that recurring dream. Immediately after, he felt loss, failure, and hate. He always thought about the murder he could have prevented, and the murder he failed to deliver.

Everything in the dream had happened. Not in that order, but it all had happened. Almost everyone was familiar. At this moment, he saw blue-eyed Erika Mueller the clearest, felt her crushing sorrow. Then, the image shifted to the cold-blooded SS man, Martin Ulricht. The boy with the rolled-up sleeves was Manny Kroner, but the face he wanted to see the most, the woman under water, never materialized. His predominant reason for reconstructing the dream was to see her face, but she never looked at him. He had no photograph of her, and he knew no one who had known her, who could describe what she looked like. She was never discernible. Never beheld. He had lost her forever. It was his mother's face, and he couldn't remember what she looked like.

The wind and rain had ceased. He saw that a thick fog surrounded him.

Ben turned on his depth finder and saw that he was still in about thirty feet of water. His watch read 1:33—he had only slept an hour. He couldn't see more than ten feet in front of him. At night, the lake gave him a creepy feeling. His wife, Isabel, had said, "Day or night, there's something frightening about this lake that I just can't explain. Maybe it's just too deep." He had always been awestruck by its blue-green winds, its girdling mountains, its pine and rock islands, as many as there were days in the year.

He and Isabel were on a turbulent river, approaching a fork, one path calm, the other wild. Eventually, they would come together again. That's how he saw it and believed it. The current would unite them. As long as there was movement and flow, eventually there would be convergence in calm, reconciling waters.

A breeze pushed across the black waters and his boat drifted into the open, full moonlight. In the platinum light, across the glassy water, he could see the shore. He was about 300 yards out. He could see the steps leading down from Van Meer's cottage to the dock. That's when he detected a light moving along the shoreline. There was someone looking inside Van Meer's boat. It was a man in a white shirt and an orange vest. Was it Van Meer?

Because the bow of his boat was near the edge of the fog, Ben feared he would be spotted if the man glanced out at the lake. He pulled at the anchor rope, which drew the boat into the fog. When he was almost out of sight, he quietly pulled up the anchor and started to paddle his boat deeper into the cover. As his bow retreated into the white mist, a paddle stroke slapped and splashed the water. Ben wondered if the man in the *MANNY A* glanced in his direction. He didn't think he could be spotted; his boat was in the fog.

Starting his engine would give him away. Hidden, he waited.

On shore, an engine started. Ben immediately tried to start his, but it wouldn't catch. He stopped trying and listened. He couldn't see, but he believed a boat was moving slowly back and forth along the wall of fog. Then, the engine shut off, and Ben saw a yellow beam of light probe the mist. Quietly, he paddled deeper in and out of reach of the light. Then he stopped and waited.

The engine started again. He saw the yellow beam of the fog light. The other boat was coming in, looking for him. Ben tried his ignition again. The motor kicked on. Slowly, he backed away from the light. He knew he would be heard if the other boat suddenly turned its motor off. He swung around and headed north, staying in the fog.

He knew the lake. He knew the shoals and rocks and could navigate it blindfolded. Twenty minutes later, he turned west and broke out of the mist into the moonlight.

The lake gleamed like polished coal. In the girdling black mirror of the water, a stalking moon slinked along, a tracking sentry on his starboard flank. Ben looked back regularly to see if he was followed but saw only the wake of his boat dipping under the wall of fog behind him.

He tied off at the Hague public dock, scrambled into his cuddy, crawled into his sleeping back, and once again tried to fall asleep. But seeing the owner of the *MANNY A* face-to-face broke his slumber into fitful segments. Could the man be Hans Kroner? That's all he thought about. Over and over, he tried to put it out of mind, but sleep did not come.

Chapter 5

Over the past several years, Ben had traveled to South and Central

America, and just three weeks ago he had gone to Mexico because the

Israeli Nazi hunters said they had cornered "Kroner." They needed Ben to

make the identification before they snatched him and hauled him off to

Israel to stand trial for war crimes. Every trip had ended in failure. The

suspected Kroner always dodged abduction. Ben had unceasingly believed

Kroner was dead, but Hannah Zar had repeatedly unfurled evidence that he

could be alive.

And now, Kroner had possibly shown up in Ben's own backyard. And

if it was Kroner, if it was the absentia death sentence of the Nuremberg

War Crimes Tribunal that Kroner had escaped, Ben might be forced to

deliver. Ben could have called Hannah Zar, and she would have come with

her entire Israeli team but this time he wanted no help. He wanted to do

this alone.

Ben still found it incredible that Kroner might be living on a lake that

he regularly fished over the past few years.

Chapter 6

Ben stared at the brightening open hatchway of the cuddy and saw that the
fog had lifted, and that the morning would be calm and sunny. His
thoughts were a blur; a swirl of dissolving images from the dream sank
into the irretrievable abyss of his subconscious.

Ben switched on the cuddy light and searched for something to eat.
There was a Snickers bar lying across one of the dividers of an open tackle
box. As he ate it, he removed from his shirt pocket the three photographs
he had taken from Van Meer's cottage. On top was the photo dated 1964,
of Van Meer in a black turtleneck sweater standing on a boat. Ben recalled
an image from his youth: a man with flinty eyes, straight blond hair,
leathery lips, a combative voice, and an unidentifiable emollient or balm on
his skin. The dark-haired man in the picture looked nothing like the man
Ben remembered. He tried to imagine the face without the beard, but the
image didn't match his recollection.

He scrutinized Van Meer's face on the photo dated 1975, just three
years ago, and compared it to the photo dated 1964. Except for the age
difference, it was the same man, but there was no likeness to the face Ben
had last seen on a cold Christmas morning in 1944.

He studied the picture of the boy and the puppy and speculated on who they were. He had stolen that photo because the date on the back, November 14, 1931, was his three year birthday, and the puppy looked like Rumpel, the gray and black Alsatian he had known as a child, whose lineage was the same as Hitler's shepherd, Blondie, a bloodline he had been reminded about regularly.

From outside, he heard a familiar voice. "Hey, Stone Heart, drop your frog and hit the deck."

Ben slid the photos inside his shirt and crawled out of the cuddy.

On the dock was his friend, Tommy Heno, a pureblooded Mohawk Indian, a local building contractor and fishing partner, standing there grinning under a Ford Thunderbird baseball hat out of which hung a long, black ponytail.

"Hi, Tommy."

"Not yet." Tommy cracked a smile with his askew teeth lined up like abandoned tombstones. "Caffeine trumps liquor at this time of day." Tommy handed Ben a Styrofoam cup. "Got some real jolt for you, buddy. It ain't that kappogino crap you city sports eat with a silver spoon. This is real jumper wire American."

"Thanks." Ben took the coffee and a saran-wrapped, peanut-buttered hard roll.

"Hey, you are one crazy sonofabitch, goin' out yesterday. Saw you comin' in and then do a one-eight-zero and go back out after that slick mahogany hull that almost rammed you. What happened?"

Ben glanced around and saw that the sky had cleared up, unlike Tommy's lined face, which looked like a smashed windshield.

Tommy lifted a veiny arm tattooed with a winged skeleton sitting on a Harley riding up the cleft of a fat lady's behind and pointed at the lake.

"Why did you chase that guy? What were you gonna' do·when you caught the mother, sink him for having poor marine etiquette?"

"I just wanted to find out where he was going. Ever see him before?"

"Yeah, over at Dale's Diner. He's new. Owns a camp over on the east side. Usually has a fat guy with him. Tall, skinny guy with fat guy tailing along. Never talked to either one of them. GQ type, you know—clean fingernails and ascots. The type that gives me the Technicolor yawn. Maybe they're a couple old fairies who slap each other's monkeys. And they ain't native sons, either. Talk funny—foreign funny. Everybody but the redskin native is a foreigner to me." Tommy took off his baseball hat, scratched his thick, black hair, and looked out at the lake. "What's going on out there on my waters?"

Ben picked up the binoculars and looked across the lake. "I don't know what's going on, Tommy. Not yet," Ben said as he peered through the lenses and found the camp on the east shore of the lake. He saw the limping man walk down to the lake and climb in the *MANNY A*.

"Untie the lines, Tommy. Push me off."

"Need some company?" Tommy smiled as he pulled out a pint of Southern Comfort, screwed off the top, and poured a gurgle into his coffee.

"I'll catch you later." Ben cranked over the motor as Tommy threw the lines in the boat. Ben pulled away from the dock. He looked across the lake and saw the *MANNY A* coming in his direction. He'd meet it out there in the middle of the lake to discover the truth. Or uncover a lie. Was Van Meer really Hans Kroner, the Nazi war criminal who had murdered Sarah Henkel, Ben's mother?

Chapter 7

Ben knew he would intercept Van Meer somewhere in the middle of Lake

George. He saw that the *MANNY A* was heading in the direction of the

dock where Tommy Heno was still standing.

Moments later, Ben saw the *MANNY A*'s wake fade and die. He knew

the boat had run out of gas, because last night he had siphoned it out and

into a five-gallon can, then emptied it into his boat, *Drifter*. Three trips had

done the job, leaving only a trace of gas in the *MANNY A*'s tank.

As Ben steered toward the Lyman, he heard three blasts of the horn and

saw the *MANNY A*'s pilot wave to him. It was Van Meer. Ben's heart raced

as he moved steadily toward the vessel. He saw that there were no other

boats in the vicinity.

The anticipation of hearing the man speak and seeing his face in the

bright sunshine mounted. Ben's whole body tightened. When he was

alongside, his voice cracked as he asked, "Need some help?"

"I am out of gas," the man said. "I topped off the tank yesterday. I just

don't understand what happened to nearly ten gallons of gasoline. I must

have a leak."

He spoke with an accent that sounded German, an intonation and

inflection that was familiar to Ben. His eyes were lapidary, steady, directly on Ben. There was nothing recognizable about the voice or the face. No familiar jeers or razored looks. Nothing at all. This man's demeanor and sound was soft and well mannered, not arrogant or incensed.

"We can pump gas from my tank into yours," Ben said. "Do you have a can?"

"I'm afraid not. Thank you for helping me. I'm Pieter Van Meer."

"Ben Steinhardt."

Ben felt a soft, creamy hand give him a tight shake. In the light, Van Meer looked quite good for his age, which Ben guessed to be late sixties, maybe seventy. The light blue, cotton turtleneck sweater and loose-fitting khaki pants concealed a stilted frame. There was no fat and very little flesh behind his tight, slightly calcified facial skin. Other than the limp, there was no physical revelation, not in a facial cast or in the sound of his voice. This man bore no resemblance to the one Ben held in his memory, but he did look like someone he had seen somewhere. A public face, perhaps, a politician or an actor.

"Let me see what I have." Ben crawled into his cuddy. He quickly came out with a plastic bait bucket and an oil extraction hand pump with a long, rubber hose—the same one he had used last night to pump gas out of Van Meer's boat. He unscrewed *Drifter*'s gas cap and started to pump gas into a bait bucket.

"Thank you so much," Van Meer said as he poured the gas into the Lyman's tank through a funnel.

"You have a very nice boat," Ben said.

"It was made in 1948. I found it at a garage sale and had it restored."

"I detect an accent. What is it?"

"Dutch."

"How long have you been in America?" Ben asked.

"1950. And your heritage is…?"

"German."

"Ah, yes, you have slight accent also." Van Meer looked up as he poured gasoline into his tank and spilled some on his deck. "You also have Germanic features." He found a rag and started to wipe up the spilled gasoline.

The gasoline fumes roused a memory from 1944. Ben was fifteen years old, hiding in the basement of a house in Dresden, looking through a small, sooty window. It had happened suddenly. They had heard the thud of boots coming up the stairs. His mother had told him to escape down the back stairs and go hide in the cellar of the empty house next door.

Through the dark glass of the cellar window, he could see SS Sturmbannführer Martin Ulricht standing next to a military truck, holding a truncheon, pushing and hitting anyone who moved too slowly. Two soldiers were shoving his mother into the back of a truck. The helping hands of her family reached out from the black opening and pulled her up. A soldier poured gas into the truck's tank and spilled some on the street. His mother's dark eyes found him behind the translucent charcoal, in the subterranean safety of the basement. The quick motion of her hand was a familiar warning: stay back, hide, don't come out.

Then, the truck pulled away and Ben rubbed the glass to see her, but she was out of sight. He ran out to the street, but the truck and the soldiers were gone. As the smell of the spilled gasoline entered his nostrils, an SS trooper grabbed him from behind. He saw the truck coming back down the street.

Van Meer finished pouring the gas, screwed on the cap, and removed his wallet. "I want to pay you for the gas, for your trouble."

"How about breakfast?" Ben suggested. "Have you had it?"

"That is precisely where I was going."

"Good."

"Only on one condition," Van Meer insisted. "I will pay. You helped me, now I want to return that assistance."

They tied off at the Hague public dock on the west side of the lake. After climbing over the gunnel, Van Meer pulled out a black cane stuck in a rod holder. His limp was very conspicuous for a few steps, then became less noticeable as he moved along, using a black cane at irregular intervals.

Dale's Diner was in the small town of Hague, a couple hundred yards from the dock. Ben glanced back at the transom of Van Meer's boat and didn't believe that the distinctive shape of each letter in *MANNY A* could have been written by anyone else but Kroner. Kroner had personally drawn and painted that exact type of script on the original *MANNY A*. The spirals on the first and last letters were exactly the same.

Chapter 8

As they silently walked toward the diner single file on the narrow

sidewalk, Ben recalled a meeting with Nazi hunter Hannah Zar almost ten

years ago.

"We have a lot in common," said the beleaguered woman in her sixties

as she opened a pack of Camels.

"What's that?" Ben asked.

"Your mother, Sarah Henkel, who was my friend in Germany before

the war. That's one thing. The other is our common enemies, Hans Kroner

and Martin Ulricht."

"They're dead."

Hannah pulled on the Camel eagerly. "I have just received new

information. Kroner and Ulricht could be very much alive."

"That's not possible," Ben said. "In 1948, a U.S. Army captain showed

me a report that said Kroner and Ulricht were killed in the last days of the

war in a Russian POW camp."

"Did a Captain Billy James show you that?"

"Yes."

"The report was fake. Under an operation known as Bring in the Brains,

hundreds, maybe thousands of Nazi scientists were brought to the United

States to work on the rocket and jet plane programs. Captain James was responsible for getting certain SS officers new identities and American citizenships. The FBI also needed to know communist tactics, and Kroner and Ulricht were put on the list as scientists. Since Kroner was a chemist, that worked. James had no intention of turning Kroner and Ulricht over to the FBI, so he showed the Bureau that same report about their death. We just learned from the Soviets that Kroner and Ulricht are still on their wanted list, that they had never been in a Soviet prison camp, and there was no Soviet report about them getting killed. James made all that up so that he could make Kroner and Ulricht vanish completely."

"Why?"

"James did it for money. A lot of money that Kroner and Ulricht had. We tried to find Captain James to ask him about them. We were a few years too late. James had been shot to death in 1948 in his remote cabin in the Louisiana bayou country the same year Kroner and Ulricht arrived in the United States. In James's bank safe deposit box, the police found a bag of jewels. That was the payment from Kroner and Ulricht for getting them into the U.S. We believe they killed James to wipe out the only person who knew their identities."

While eating Western omelets and drinking coffee, Pieter Van Meer told Ben about his widowhood. "My wife has been dead two years now. I'm still in shock. She was young. Only sixty when she passed on. Cancer." He sighed. "Thank God I have my daughter, Mandy. She is married and lives in California. So, I see her only on Christmas and she visits me in the summer."

Van Meer drank his coffee quickly, making a slight sucking sound with every sip. The noise rankled Ben; he thought he remembered Kroner making that sound when he drank coffee.

"Your boat is named *Manny*, not *Mandy?* Or did I read the lettering wrong?"

"This is the story." Van Meer smiled and leaned forward, excited. "You see, my daughter's full name is Amanda. Mandy for short. Somehow Manny became her nickname."

"What does the 'A' stand for?"

"My late wife's name was Audrey. That's why we named it the *MANNY A*. Your boat has a melancholy, lonely name. *Drifter*."

"That was its name when I bought it. Drifting is a fishing tactic. Besides, it's bad luck to change a boat's name."

The white beard only softened the granite jaw, but it was there—a feature Ben remembered. Pieter Van Meer was a man with well-bred manners. He ate like a European, knife in the right hand, fork in the left, and didn't switch them like an American. He chewed in small bites with his mouth closed and dabbed his lips with the napkin regularly, almost excessively.

Halfway through the meal, Van Meer picked up his black cane and went to the bathroom.

Tommy walked over. "How you makin' out? Ain't that the guy who almost rammed you? This a peace pipe powwow I'm spectating?"

"I don't know what it is exactly, Tommy. Not yet."

"Oh, I didn't get a chance to tell you the latest on that Agent Orange class action. Now there's enough red tape out there to reach the moon. Our flyboys couldn't tell us grunts apart from the foliage. And the way things are going, I figure my great-grandchildren should collect by the time they're on Social Security. Don't you just love our government? They send us off to fight for freedom and democracy and don't tell us that it's not their intention to even win the fucking war. And then to top it off, they spray us with a defoliant that gives us diseases they don't even have names for, and then they say it wasn't Orange that did it. Shit. Don't piss on my back and tell me it's raining."

"Here he comes, Tommy."

"The government's slimier than the bottom of the Hudson," Tommy muttered. He went back to the counter and sat down.

Van Meer slid into the booth slowly. "Is that man a friend of yours?"

"Yeah. He's a local contractor. We fish together. He's a Vietnam vet."

Van Meer held the coffee cup to his lips. "He has an interesting face."

"He's a pure-blooded Mohawk Indian."

"But Tommy is not a typical Indian name."

"His full name is Tom Tom Heno   Tom tom, the drum. Heno is the Iroquois God of Thunder. He says his family never left the banks of this lake. He has papers that prove Mohawk ownership, showing it was left to them before the broken treaties of the late 1700s, when the white man swindled and seized the rest of State of New York from the natives.

"To rile the rich local gentry, Tommy says he's going to let the Mohawk Nation annex his land and open a casino but would ditch the idea if all motorboats were banned on the lake. He's raising hell to get the locals to pass stricter emissions laws to keep the lake clean. Tommy knows that the annexation-casino idea doesn't have a chance. This land is subject to the laws of New York State, not the Mohawk Nation. He just likes to let people know the Indians are still here, even after the attempted genocide by the white invaders."

"Do you have a family?"

Ben told Van Meer that he had separated from his wife recently and they had two kids, a boy of nine and a girl of seven. He took out his wallet and showed him a photograph of Isabel, Max Jr., and Maria.

As Van Meer glanced at the photo, he said, "Ah, ja, ja, your wife is very beautiful."

"Isabel is Cuban."

"Americans are truly an amalgamation. Was she a native Cuban?"

"Yes."

"I hope you can be reconciled."

"Me too."

"How long have you been separated?"

"About three weeks."

Van Meer searched his pockets, and then got up, "I have to go back to the boat to get my pills. They must have fallen out when I was refueling. Darn pills. Can't live without them."

As Van Meer tottered away, Ben's memory slid back ten years to 1968, to a Miami Beach country club.

Chapter 9

The barmaid wore a glittering, aquamarine outfit that looked more like a chemise than something you wore to work. It was tight, salacious, and provocative. Her black hair was abundant and curly. She had warm, brown eyes. The outfit clung to her fawn skin like iridescent scales to a sleek tropical fish.

Ben watched her fluid movements behind the bar, twisting, turning, pouring, mixing, shaking, back and forth on the terrazzo on clicking, turquoise spiked heels, doing her trade Terpsichore, her barmaid bolero to a bossa nova beat coming from the speakers above the bar.

As she handed him a margarita, she said, "Por favor, guapo."

"Muchas gracias, bonita."

"Hey gringo, you trying to score points with that baby-talk Spanish?"

"Sure. Aren't you?"

"Sorry, guapo, I'm just peddling booze."

"So my Spanish really sounds like baby-talk?"

"It's elementary. What can I say?"

"In the Bronx, I learned that life really doesn't get much better than what's elementary."

"Hey!" someone shouted. "Down this way, honey."

"Verdad?" she said, walking off to take the order.

Later, she walked past Ben and saw that his margarita glass was empty. "Another?"

When she gave him the drink, she leaned her elbows on the bar and asked, "So, how much Spanish do you know?"

"Sometimes just enough to get me into trouble."

"Is that so? Como se llama?"

"Ben. And yours?"

"Isabel."

It was just past midnight when Isabel came out of the country club. She had accepted Ben's invitation to go out for a drink and show him around Miami. She had changed into a black skirt and a pink halter-top.

"Had to shed that pearly snakeskin," she said. That's for Carnival in Rio or the Malecon in Havana. Really, it's for the regular old gringos here at the club. Bar bait. Moves the booze and gets the tips."

"It must also elevate their heartbeat. Mine went right off the scale."

"What's your full name, hombre?"

"Ben Steinhardt."

"Isabel Navarro. Let's take my car. I like the top down."

In a 1965 red Sting Ray, Isabel drove down Calle Ocho. In Little Havana, she said, "In March, we have a huge festival here. Thousands of people dance in the streets, stay up all night, and get drunk. It's the largest and wildest Latin party in the States. That's Navarro's, my family's restaurant." She pointed at a white stucco building with an orange Spanish tile roof and bougainvillea vines creeping across the walls, their large, magenta bracts grasping inconspicuous flowers. "My sister and brothers run it. I tend bar there sometimes."

"Same outfit as before?"

"Are you crazy? Navarro's is a long, black, lace dress kind of place with classical Spanish guitars and waiters in flamenco tuxes."

"Hey, the body bracelet looked great on you."

"Yeah, I bet it did. I need help to get in and out of it." She laughed and nudged him with her elbow. "I know what you're thinking. Erase that picture. I am not that kind of a girl. Although your first impression of me, because of that glitzy outfit, must have been, what, 'This is a slutty woman asking for it?' Right?"

"It was a costume for the role you had to play behind the bar. I didn't think you were trashy at all."

"Men are drawn to that look. What makes you different?"

"I'm not. Okay, I was drawn. And now that you're no longer in it, I'm still captivated. Anyway, what's wrong with being attracted to a glitzy outfit on a body that can wear it?"

"Nada, just don't think the glitz covers trash. Not on this chica." She skidded to a stop and parallel parked into a tight spot.

The small club was crowded with Cubans, the confined dance floor a rhythmic gyration of swaying and sweating couples dancing to a Perez Prado record. Tables were packed with slick black-haired men in silk shirts and women in tight, short skirts. Mobs of beer bottles, rum and Cokes, and margaritas on could spend a night with teetered on the edges of spiky-legged, black iron tables. The place was dripping and perspiring with glistening, swarthy bodies.

Isabel looked around and found two empty chairs near someone she knew. Her introductions were lost in music, laughter, and loud talk. Ben heard Hernando something and Perez somebody and Rosa so and so.

Rosa, a bogus blonde with thick, scarlet lips gave Isabel a white gardenia. "What I need two for?" Laughed syrupy Rosa.

Her maudlin boyfriend, Hernando, said, "Why do you give her that one? I paid five bucks for it."

"I keep the one you got from the dumpster behind the flower shop. I give my friend the one without the fly shit on the petals."

"Gracias, Rosalita." Isabel stuck the waxy blossom in her hair and asked Ben, "Want to dance?"

"I don't tango."

"That's not the tango. It's the habanera, an old Cuban dance. It's nice, no? Hey, what happened to the man who liked elementary things? Dancing is not one of them?"

"When it comes to dancing, I am pathetic."

Hernado interrupted, "The fucking Argentinos stole the habanera from the Cubans, altered it, and called it the tango. The bendejos in Argentina do the tango like maracones."

"Come on," Isabel said. "It's not hard at all."

Rosa said, "What's the matter with you, guapo, go, go. The woman wants to dance."

Isabel held out her hand. Her enticing eyes said *I want to know you, feel you move with me,* made Ben take her hand while he could only mutter, "I don't habanera either."

He was a naturally poor dancer. She poked fun at him. "Are all you Anglos so stiff? Let loose. No one cares if you make a fool of yourself. Look at that guy over there—he's stepping on her toes, but his woman's sexy smile is only for him. Latin women demand that their men dance. They don't care if they're not good."

A drink and another attempt later, Isabel said, "See. A few missed steps, off-balance glides, and stubbed toes, and you got it. I'll be in intensive care, but you will be the Latino Fred Astaire."

After a few more dances, they went out to a patio to cool off. The music was now like the night around them—in the steamy background, quelled by distance. The habanera remained with Ben like a sweet dream. They placed their drinks on a cracked stucco wall. Below was an indolent canal that led out to the Intercostal. They were confined by the night and the water. Beyond the palms were faint, tepid stars. Through the habanera, Ben had felt Isabel's fundamental cadence, relished her touch and the brush of her legs, felt her soft, embracing arms, and in their moving and shifting alliance, he had been lost in the redolence of the ambrosial gardenia in her hair.

He took her hand. Her dark eyes pulled him towards her. Speech with its wanting words ebbed. There was something sweeter and deeper in the motion of his descent and her accessible, open stillness.

The thrashing and splashing of water and a yelp stopped him, distracted her. Isabel turned around and peered over the wall down at the dark canal. "Gator! Picked off a white poodle with a red bow around its head. I saw it. Man, that's Cuba down there in the canal."

He started to ask how, but she cut him off. "The dog's look was his last, like the Cuban people. The gator was Fidel. You never see him kill, but he's chopping up opposition all the time."

He looked down and neither saw nor heard anything.

"I'm telling you, that's Cuba down there in the canal," she repeated. Her look was inflexible, angry. "Deadly under the surface. You hear things afterwards, but never see it happen. People just vanish. That dog must have pissed on Fidel's hydrant."

She took a long gulp of her sweating Margarita. "I was fifteen years old when Fidel took over. We got out of Cuba a few days before Batista's fall. My father had friends in Miami. He came here with some money, bought an old restaurant, fixed it up, expanded it, and now it's the best Spanish and Cuban food in Florida. Oh, this you'll find interesting." The hard sadness dissipated with her bright smile as she turned her back to the canal. "Get this. For the past two years on August 13, Navarro's gets a big Cuban-style paella order to go. A limo arrives to pick it up. My sister told me that the limo drives directly to Miami International, then flies off in a private jet that eventually winds up in Havana. August 13 is Fidel's birthday. I think we are catering Fidel's birthday and can't advertise it because the Cubans of Miami would hate us if they got wind of it."

"Poison the paella and they will love you."

She laughed and touched his arm. "I wish it were so easy to kill Fidel. The CIA and the Mafia couldn't do it."

"What's Cuban paella? How is it different from Spanish?"

"Cuban is seafood with every bite. Spanish is stingy on the seafood. A lot of rice."

Later, they were driving through Miami. Isabel made sharp turns, squealing tires, leaning into him, hair flying back, one leg stamping the clutch, the other hitting the brake and driving into the accelerator like she wanted it to go through the floor, dominating the stubby chrome shifter.

"Hold on," she said. The tires squealed through a ninety-degree turn. "Damn Vettes got jello for suspension."

She told Ben she took classes at Miami U. "I'm sick of peddling liquor. I want to do counseling right here in Little Havana. Most Latinos are hard workers. I want to help the new people arriving from South of the border."

When she asked him what he did, he told her he owned an architectural/construction business in Saratoga, New York.

"I'm down here for a builder's convention and visiting my grandfather."

"Would you like to see some of Miami's really interesting architecture?" she asked.

"Only burglars do house tours at three in the morning."

"Doesn't Miami look better now than in the daylight? I like the night." She took a deep breath. "Everything is better at night. The night is full of enigmas."

They drove into the cryptic and densely verdant Coconut Grove with its unusual building styles. Next, they were in Coral Gables, where the streets and avenues were named after Spanish cities and the houses had a Mediterranean look. Isabel was right—the streets were deserted and verdant, the houses obfuscated by fences and foliage and shadows. Even some of the garish architectural designs didn't look too bad at night. Especially the shadowy landscaping, the leafy, dark places.

On their second date, she told him that her husband had been killed in an auto accident five years ago.

"I'm sorry." Ben said. "I was also married, but it didn't last. Four months."

"My God, Ben. Four months? What happened?"

"She was a survivor of the Holocaust, had lost her whole family in a death camp. We shared too many horrible memories. We could not help each other."

On Ben's last night in Miami, Isabel took him out to Key Largo. They stopped along the water and watched a sailboat make for port, pushed by the winds of an approaching storm. She put the top up on the Corvette as it started to rain. When she reached across to show him how the temperamental window handle worked, he kissed her on the cheek. She turned her mouth to his quickly, then pulled away.

"I have this feeling," Ben said. "Got it instantly almost, got it about a week ago at a bar over a margarita. I have it right now. Butterflies in my stomach. Do you know what I'm talking about?"

"Yeah, I know about that feeling. Your heart is having a love seizure. It will pass." Then her smile changed from jest to diffidence. She was unguarded and captivated. "Am I going to have a problem here?"

"You are."

They checked in at the Waldorf Towers, a white, purple, and yellow art deco hotel in Miami Beach. The night was stormy. Wind and rain battered the coast. Beyond the plate glass, the whipped palms shed their thrashing fronds, their stiff trunks muscular and resilient in the lashing gale.

She was standing behind him and running her fingers down his chest, turning him, descending to the mattress they had dragged over in front of the rain-splattered glass, taking him again, while beyond the drenched, opalescent shield, the salty waters of the Atlantic slammed inland.

In the morning, Ben watched Isabel walk over to the window.

"You know what?" he said, stepping up beside her and feeling the warmth of the rising sun radiating through the plate glass.

"What, Ben?"

"I love saying your name. Isabel Navarro. It rolls off like a moonbeam across tropical waves."

"Slow down, Ben. Moonbeams and tropical waves? You're sailing on some fairytale sea."

"Are you asking me to stop? We're in it, Isabel. The wind is too good not to take. We're a couple of shooting stars doing the habanera around the sun."

He loved toying with festooned images. He sensed she was entertained by them.

Her eyes darkened. "I'm a little scared of my feelings. Shocked almost."

"For two people who just met, there's something happening," he said. "This is more than just adorned words and mad passion. Something good and true is happening. Am I right?"

"Si. You are."

Ben had gone back to Saratoga to finish a home he was building. He flew down to Florida a few times. She flew up to visit him once. A few months later, Ben said to Isabel, "I want you to meet my best man."

It was bridge night at Max Steinhardt's when Ben and Isabel arrived.

Max, Ben's grandfather, put his arm around him. "Hadn't been for Ben, I'd be a dead man. He saved my life."

"We saved each other," Ben said.

Isabel was about to ask, "How?" but was interrupted.

"Lucky for God," one of the bridge players said. "If Max was in heaven, God would get ulcers."

"So who says Max is going to heaven?"

"I've been to hell already," Max said. "God wouldn't send me back."

"Who says there even is a God?" one of the men said.

"There's a God all right," Max said. "You know why? The Jews are still here. All the other ancient civilizations, God has knocked out into oblivion—the Romans, the Huns, the Carthaginians, the Phoenicians, all of them. Only the Jews have survived. We haven been hit hard throughout history, but we keep surviving. Why? Is God trying to teach us something?"

Milton, Max's closest friend, said, "Maxie, you're the only Jew I know who doesn't have a sense of humor. Heaven's a happy place. No place for you. You're going to hell for sure."

"So, Miltie my friend, you think they have humor in heaven?" Max said. "All Methodists and Presbyterians up there. You ever meet a funny one?"

"Never. You're right. The jokes gotta be in hell."

"Ain't no humor in hell, either. When you're dead, all the jokes are over. Anyway, the SS killed my sense of humor."

Milton stuck a long cigar in his mouth. "That SS business was thirty years ago. You gotta let that go."

"You're an ignorant schmuck, Milt. You grow up in nice, nice America, and you got the balls to tell me to let the Holocaust go. The Holocaust took my entire family except for my grandson, Ben. Your biggest trauma, Milt, was your mother forcing you to eat chicken soup when you were a kid. You carry the chicken soup horror around with you your entire life; even spend a few years with the shrink to help you get over it. And after all that therapy, you still can't let the chicken soup horror go. And you think I should let the Holocaust go. The Holocaust, Milt? To you, it's the same as that chicken soup? I can never let the Holocaust go because it won't let me go. And I don't want it to. It's my past, present, and future. It's me. It commands me and it owns me. It's what I hear and see and smell and think. It's the blood that runs through me. It's what makes my heartbeat, what directs my thinking and praying and dreaming and shitting and screwing. The Holocaust is undeniable proof that there is a God. The Holocaust brought the Jews to the brink of destruction—but only the brink. We were saved for another day. God wanted us back in Israel and the Holocaust did it. He sent us back to a place that is surrounded by enemies who want to destroy us. Can't figure God. When you understand just some of that, Milt, you will stop being a schmuck."

"Sorry, Max," Milt said. "Too many whiskey sours."

When Isabel and Ben were in the car driving away, she asked, "How did you save your grandfather's life?"

"It's a long story."

"I want to hear it."

He told her most of it, leaving out feelings he had shared only with his grandfather.

A few months later, Isabel and Ben got married in a small church in Miami's Little Havana. Max was his best man. The reception was in her family's restaurant.

Ten years after their wedding, Isabel and their two kids were gone.

Chapter 10

Van Meer hobbled back to the diner from his boat, opened the pill bottle, took two, and asked, "I was thinking as I was walking back. I hope you are staying in touch with your wife?"

"We are." He had spoken to Isabel about the kids, nothing about getting back together. It had been a fractional conversation. Unfinished thoughts and fragmented assessments skirted the edge of the connection that was now damaged—temporarily, Ben hoped. There was her cool exasperation, her reproaches. They circled each other's defenses, trying to get close again. With muted passion, they said they loved each other. But in the tone of their goodbye, there was a wayward outrider. They would stay separated for a while yet.

The last time he saw Isabel was three weeks ago. He had been packing to go with Hannah Zar to Mexico City. Hannah had an address, name, and photograph. "We got him," she said. A contingent of Israeli agents would make the Eichmann-style extraction once Ben made the positive identification.

As he packed, Isabel came into the doorway and stood with her hands on her hips, in her helical Latina stance he knew only too well.

"Where now, Ben?" she asked. Demanded.

"Mexico City. They found him."

"Found who, Ben? Who did Hannah Zar find this time? Elvis?" Her voice was rising, heating up.

"You know who. Him. Kroner."

"Let me guess. You're the only one who can identify him?"

"That's right. When I was sixteen, I saw Kroner up close."

"That was more than thirty years ago. Don't you think he'll have changed? Like, beyond recognition or identification? Don't they have fingerprints to match? Or photographs? Or dental records? Or maybe your own memory has changed."

"My memory is very, very clear. The Israelis have only me."

She came over to the bed where Ben was sitting and kneeled in front of him. "Ben, over the past year, you have been away more than you have been home. You have missed birthday parties, recitals, holidays, everyday things."

"I made your birthday."

"Yeah, but you missed our tenth."

"I sent flowers."

"FTD carnations."

"The shop was out of red roses."

"I like daffodils and tulips. Remember?"

"Right. I'll get it right. I'll make it up."

"Don't go on this trip. I know you want to get Kroner. You're obsessed with it. I'm asking you to let Hannah and her people do it some other way. Tell her to find another witness. You have been away too much. You stay away too long. There's no money coming in. We're falling apart."

"I'm really sorry. This is the last time."

"No. Absolutely not. You can't go. You promised that the last time you went."

"This time they got him. I have to go."

"No. They had him the last time." She sprang to her feet. "No, no, no. You're not going."

Isabel walked out of the room, muttering, "No más, no más." Ben heard the car door slam and tires squeal.

He drove to the airport alone. When he got to Mexico City, Kroner was gone. He had slipped around the surveillance, as he had on countless other trips to faraway places. When Ben got home, Isabel and the kids were also gone.

Ben had told her that Kroner had murdered his mother. He had been too ashamed to tell her that Kroner was his father. Or that Ben Steinhardt was an assumed name—that his real name was Manfred Aaron Kroner.

Chapter 11

"Keep the communication lines open and be patient," Van Meer said.
"Perhaps the time apart will draw you back together."

"I hope I didn't screw up a damn fine marriage."

"If you don't mind my asking, what did you do that was so terrible?"

"I just placed some personal, private matters above my family and marriage," Ben said as he looked at Van Meer. Was this the same man who had recently been photographed in Mexico City? In that photograph, there was a man with long white hair in a ponytail, a white beard, and large, dark sunglasses. Van Meer didn't look like that man. Of course, if they had arrested the man in Mexico, they would have had a face-to-face encounter. The dark glasses would have been off and the hair could have been a wig. They had failed to get that closer look.

Van Meer looked straight at Ben as he slurped his coffee. "Our past histories are cumbersome rucksacks. Getting along takes diplomacy, compromises. It's not easy to strike a balance between personalities. Who will figure out the dynamics? That is always the question. I think a trailblazer is needed in any successful venture, be it running a country, a business, or a marriage. Anyway, I think it's easier to predict the weather than who will succeed in matrimony. Men and women are too different to confine to a contract for a long duration."

Ben nodded in agreement.

"Do you live near the lake?" Van Meer asked.

"I live in Saratoga. How about yourself? Is your permanent home on the lake?"

"This is it. Right here on the lake."

"How long have you been here?"

"This is the first year," Van Meer said.

"Do you rent?"

"No, I bought a place this spring."

As Van Meer stepped into his boat, he tripped but caught himself on the gunwale. "It's my damn leg."

"What's wrong with it?"

"From the knee down it's artificial. It's a prototype in prosthetics. I'm letting a European company try one out on me. In fact, I sent them suggestions on the electronic circuitry needed for something like this and they came up with the idea I am using now. Sensors implanted in it pick up temperature and pressure. The electronic pulses go to nerve endings, and then to the brain where they are experienced. When I walk, I actually feel the pressure of my foot on the ground."

"I did detect a limp when you got out of your boat. But you seem to move around as if you have two good legs. How did you lose it?"

"During one of the Allied air raids on Rotterdam, the building I worked in collapsed and a beam fell on my leg. I was trapped for days, got gangrene, and part of the leg had to be amputated. It seems to cramp up every now and then above the knee."

"How do you know so much about electronics?"

"I'm a chemical and electrical engineer. My hobby is inventing. All kinds of gadgets. Most of them worthless."

Ben also recalled that Kroner had been an amateur inventor of toys and children's science experiments. "It's a beautiful day," he said. "Would you like to go fishing with me for a few hours?"

Van Meer accepted.

Ben helped him climb into his boat and take a seat on an aft bench.

"Your boat is well-equipped. What are all these electronic devices?" Van Meer asked.

"Depth sounders, fish finders, Loran. Toys for navigation and fishing."

"There are too many wires and switches and sonar sensors. How do you find the time to enjoy the water and the surrounding scenery?"

"Actually, it gives me more time. I just push the buttons and the fish jump into my boat."

"Scaled, deboned, and poached?"

Ben smiled and pointed at a tour boat steaming northward. "That's the *Lac du Saint Sacrament.*"

"Isn't that also the original name of this lake?"

"Lac du Saint Sacrament was the name given to the lake by its European discoverer, Jesuit Father Jogues, back in the sixteen hundreds. The native name was Andiatarocte."

"An-dia-ta-roc-te." Van Meer said each syllable deferentially. "What does it mean?"

"'End of the Waters.'"

"So when did it become Lake George?"

"It was named that by the British in the seventeen hundreds."

"When the French renamed the lake, they were driven out," Van Meer said. "So were the British after renaming the lake. It's clearly bad luck to rename this lake." He smiled. "Perhaps the Americans were very smart in not renaming the lake."

Ben said, "My Mohawk friend Tommy Heno believes that renaming a sacred place, changing a true name will bring bad luck to the renamer.

"He really believes that the white man has renamed too many sacred places. To him, the United States is Big Turtle Island. The Americans renamed the entire country. Therefore, they, like the French and the British, will eventually depart. When I wanted to rename my boat, Tommy told me it would bring me bad luck. So, I left it the *Drifter*."

"Really?" Van Meer said. "I feel awful now. You see, I renamed my boat."

"From what?"

"*My Last Boat*."

"To the *MANNY A*. After your daughter, Mandy?"

"Correct. For my daughter and my wife, Audrey."

Chapter 12

The sky was powder blue with high cirrus clouds, the air warm and calm and the surface like glass. But the undulations of these waters were familiar to Ben; abruptly, a brutal wind could slash and blow between the trough of enclosing mountains and churn the lake.

After they had caught one legal sized lake trout and one salmon, they headed back to the town dock to get Van Meer's boat.

As Van Meer stepped onto the dock, he said, "I'm going to gas up my boat and check if there is a leak in my tank, then go back to my cottage. I want to repay you for all your kindness. How about lunch back at my cottage? I'll cook the fish, unless you had other plans for them."

Ben tailed the *MANNY A.* across the lake. In the clear, sunlit forenoon, the eastern lakeside was not as threatening as it had been during last night's covert undertaking. The sun was now high over the mountains, shimmering on the green pine branches overhanging the dark rooftops of the small cottages hidden and scattered across the treed hillside. Above, like an ominous judge, stood a granite escarpment.

As the *MANNY A.* docked, Van Meer motioned to Ben to tie off on the other side.

The dock at Van Meer's cottage was recently constructed from pressure treated yellow pine. Its watery pores were forced out by insecticides and preservatives, the wood no longer a drive-in eatery for wood-consuming insects or decay. At the top of the mooring posts were iron brackets from which hung flowerpots crammed with impatients and vines. The steps leading up to Van Meer's wood-shingled house were made from treated lumber and inlaid red brick treads. Alongside the terraced walkway leading up to the cottage were showy white and pink begonias, recently mulched and weeded. Also flourishing in the shade of the pines was a field of pachysandra. Other than a few spots where the pachysandra was crushed and depressed, the landscaping was immaculate. Only a few brown pine needles lay across the green ground cover. There were no weeds in sight.

Van Meer stopped and picked off a pine needle and stood up some flattened pachysandra, muttering, "I wonder how that happened. It looks like a bear walked through there."

They walked up the freshly painted wooden steps and across the wood floor of an open porch. The door was unlocked. An oval brown hook rug covered a glistening oak floor. There was a TV in one corner, a small green couch, and a pine coffee table with *Newsweek*, *National Geographic*, and a Glens Falls newspaper. A faded lithograph of the Narrows on Lake George was opposite the picture window looking out over the lake, where tan drapes made a soft frame. A floor-to-ceiling bookcase stood on either side of the massive, cobblestone fireplace. An unusually high black metal spark screen girdled the tiled hearth. Ben had never seen a screen that high. Almost chest height. In one corner, some brightly painted and varnished wooden toys were neatly arranged. With the lemon yellow wall paint, the natural wood floors, and the large glass window, the room had a balmy feel.

Ben walked over to the spark screen and placed his hands on the top of the chest-high iron rail. He tested it and felt no movement. "Wow. This is really some screen. Why so high?"

"I had a big dog. A shepherd. I would put him in there when visitors came. There's a gate. He was unpredictable. When I went to the doctors or shopping, I put him in there so he wouldn't run around and scratch up the floors."

Ben thought of Rumpel.

"Where is he now?"

"He died. Old age. He was almost fifteen."

"What was his name?"

"Rudi. Rudi was his name. I should make this fish." Van Meer said walked off into the kitchen.

Ben studied the screen a little longer and saw that ceramic or glass insulators were located where the screen rails and posts met the cobblestone fireplace. They were the type used in high voltage electrical networks.

While the trout and salmon fillets sputtered in the butter next to the simmering green peas, the potatoes hummed and vibrated in the microwave. Van Meer made a sauce from mayonnaise, fresh dill, and lemon. He tore up oak leaf lettuce and whisked a dressing from sour cream, milk, fresh dill, and salt. They were sitting across the table from each other, drinking beer. After the fillets were fried, Van Meer stuck them in the freezer to chill. "Hot fish is too mushy."

The slightly tart oak leaf lettuce, sour cream, and buttermilk dressing were familiar to Ben. He hadn't had it in many years, but knew it.

Van Meer said, "Audrey and I used to rent a cabin on various lakes for two weeks each summer. When this cottage went up for sale, we bought it.

The winters are long and lonely, but I keep busy with my foul weather hobbies. I'm an amateur inventor. It's a just a hobby, though. I have never sold one of my inventions, or even got a patent. I make foolish little things for around the house.

"My daughter comes up for two weeks in the summer. I look forward to that. It is the best part of my life. This cottage will be hers when I die. Would you like to see my family album?"

Van Meer walked into the other room and came back with a photo album—the same album Ben had seen the night before. He opened it and turned the pages. "My wife was a beautiful woman. Don't you agree?"

"Yes, she was. I am sorry for your loss."

Van Meer looked away. "I'm still having a difficult time with it. She was my best friend. And this is my daughter, Mandy, and my granddaughter, Nancy. This is my son-in-law, Richard. He's a surgeon—a very good one, too. My daughter was very lucky. Of course, he has a wonderful wife. Mandy is my joy. In fact, she will be here next week." He got up. "How about some coffee?"

As Van Meer ground the coffee and filled the pot, Ben reached in his shirt pocket to take out the photographs he had pilfered the night before. He'd just slide the boy and dog photo into the album and come upon it to ask Van Meer about it. But the pictures weren't there. He checked the other pocket. Nothing. Had he slid them into his windbreaker? Or had they fallen out in the boat?

He hoped they hadn't fallen out onto the boat while they were fishing.

"That coffee smells good."

"I mix Colombian and French roast together and grind it fresh," Van Meer said.

Ben stood up. "I'm all out of smokes. I have some in the boat. I could never drink that great smelling coffee without a smoke. I'll be right back."

As he hurried down to the boat he checked his pants pockets. Empty. He stepped into his boat and looked around, then crawled into the cuddy, where he checked his wallet, the sleeping bag, and the waterproof storage box. No pictures. From the cuddy, he glanced around the deck of the boat.

Nothing. No pictures. They had to be somewhere on the boat. Could they have slid out of his pocket while he was landing the lake trout, while leaning over the boat to net one of them? That was possible; the shirt pocket had not been buttoned. But it was unlikely, because he would have seen them fall out. He glanced up the hill and saw Van Meer back away from the window.

Before Ben stepped out of the boat, he slid a sheathed fillet knife into his sock, put a rubber band around it to hold it, and went back up the hill.

The aroma of the brewing coffee absorbed the fishy odor of the kitchen. Van Meer wasn't in the kitchen when he entered. Ben called out, "Mr. Van Meer?"

The floor creaked several times. The sound came from upstairs. Was Van Meer getting the pistol? Then the toilet flushed, and Ben heard footsteps coming down the stairs.

Van Meer entered the kitchen. "Let's have that coffee now."

Ben stood up. "May I use your bathroom?"

"Ja, ja, by all means. Upstairs. Second door on the left."

As Ben passed the bedroom, he saw that the gun was no longer on the nightstand. He continued on into the bathroom. As he flushed the toilet and tucked in his shirt, the pictures fell on the floor. He had slid them inside his shirt, between his t-shirt and outer shirt, not his pocket. All three of them.

Relieved, he took the boy and dog picture and put it in his shirt pocket. The other two he slid back inside his shirt.

At the kitchen table, Ben stirred sugar into his coffee. When Van Meer went to the refrigerator to get milk, Ben slipped the baby and dog picture into the album. He wanted to see Van Meer's reaction when he saw it. Van Meer returned and sat across the table from him and drank the black coffee. His pursed lips on the rim of the cup made a slight sucking sound that annoyed Ben.

As Ben returned to leafing through the album, he saw that his fingers were trembling slightly. He pointed at one of the faces. "Your daughter Mandy as a teenager, right?"

"Yes. She's was a very bright girl." Van Meer smiled. "Now she is a genetic biologist. Her field will do great things for humanity."

"I hope so. Humanity certainly needs some help. But genetics is too sci-fi for me. I wouldn't want the future to become a human assembly line of different models."

Van Meer started to say something, then abandoned it.

Ben turned to the first blank page, then another, then the photo. Because it was loose, he picked it up and asked, "Who's the boy?"

Van Meer took the picture and glanced at it. "My brother's son." He flipped the picture over. "Yes, this is my nephew at about three years old or thereabouts. He was killed during the war. He was just a teenager."

"I'm sorry to hear that. How did he die at such a young age?"

"War kills randomly. It makes no distinctions between soldiers and children."

Van Meer put the picture down on the black page of the album and closed it slowly.

"You have a nice family," Ben said, standing up.

Van Meer nodded and smiled. "Yes, I do."

"I really have to get going. Tomorrow is a workday. I want to thank you for your hospitality."

"And I want to thank you for helping me."

Van Meer didn't walk him down to the dock; he said his leg was bothering him. They exchanged phone numbers, said goodbye in the doorway, and promised to see each other again.

Ben pushed off from Van Meer's dock. The lake was getting rougher as humid air pressed heavily down upon the water. It was early afternoon, and he heard distant thunder. The sound always reminded him of the Allied bombers approaching Dresden in February of 1945.

Looking south across the shining water, above the many islands of the Narrows, Ben saw black clouds swelling on the humpbacked horizon, shifting, grotesque shapes broiling into the thunderstorm that would hit the lake in a few hours.

As he swung *Drifter* around and moved ahead, Ben wondered if Van Meer was trying to figure out how the baby picture got from the envelope in his desk into the album. His explanation about the name *MANNY A.* sounded believable. The story about the baby picture could be true.

Was it all a coincidence—the *MANNY A.*, the limp, the German accent? A strange happenstance that had sent Ben on an insane pursuit? Van Meer was not even German. Dutch, so he had said. It was probably true. A part of Ben felt relieved that Van Meer might not be Kroner; the other part wished he was. To know the truth, Ben would have to send the two photographs still in his shirt pocket to Hannah Zar.

When he saw a familiar charter fisherman, Ben switched on his radio to Channel 68. "This is *Drifter* calling *Close Call*. Come in, *Close Call*. Over."

"Hey, Ben, got the derby in the bag yet?"

"Not even close," Ben said. "My well's empty. How about you?"

"I got a couple. I don't think they'll do. Tommy said you got a problem. Need help, just holler. *Close Call* out."

Ben moved the throttle ahead and picked up speed. About a quarter-mile from shore, the VHF radio crackled and snapped. He adjusted the squelch. "This is the *MANNY A.* calling *Drifter*. Over."

Ben picked up the mike. "This is *Drifter*. Over."

"This is the *MANNY A.* Come back, Ben, I need help. I think I'm having a heart attack."

Chapter 13

Ben tied off *Drifter* and ran up to the cottage. Van Meer was sitting in the rocking chair by the picture window. He looked pale and frightened and clutched a telephone in his lap.

"What's wrong, Mr. Van Meer?"

"Thank you for coming back." Van Meer held one hand on his chest. "I have a heart condition. I've taken my nitroglycerin pill." He pointed at the bottle on the end table.

"Did you call an ambulance?"

"No. I called my doctor's office, then I called you."

"Doctor? Don't you think you should call an ambulance? Or let me take you to the hospital in Glens Falls."

"I've had these attacks before. The pain is subsiding. Thank you for coming back. I was confused. You were close by."

"I'll drive you to a hospital. I insist."

"Thank you, but I don't think that will be necessary. The last time I went, they wouldn't let me leave for three days. I've called my doctor. It will be okay. This has happened to me a few times before. I just wanted someone here in the event I took a turn for the worse."

"I'll stay here until you're feeling better."

"I'm really grateful you came back. I didn't know where this attack was going, and I had no one to call nearby. My next-door neighbor is not home, so you were my only choice." Van Meer leaned forward in the rocker. "The coffee is still hot. Please, have a cup."

"Would you like one too?"

"Not right now."

Ben went into the kitchen, and as he poured the aromatic blend, he heard the telephone ring and Van Meer answer it at half-ring.

"Ja, ja, I'm feeling better." Then there were more yes and no answers and some questions by Van Meer, and then he said, "Yes, tomorrow at ten. I will see you then. Thank you for returning my call so promptly."

When Ben walked back into the living room, Van Meer was leaning back in the chair. "That was my doctor. He said he'd see me tomorrow." His creased brow had smoothed over. He grasped the phone in both hands, as if he were afraid someone was going to take it away from him.

"Please, sit down, Ben." He took a deep breath. "Ah, I'm feeling better. Ja, much better. It's going to be okay."

"Are you sure?"

"Ja, ja. Okay, okay. But if you could just stay a short while, I would be grateful. We can just chat a while, unless you have to go."

"I don't mind staying."

"Thank you, Ben. Because you are a builder, I do need your advice."

"If I can help, of course."

"I am considering enlarging this cottage. I would like to put on a room with a private bath, make it nicer for my daughter, and perhaps for myself later on. Where do you think is the best location, and how much will it cost?"

"You must have some idea where you want to add on."

"Oh yes, I was thinking of going off that end of the cottage."

Ben glanced at the windowless south end of the room. The fireplace was in the center, with floor-to-ceiling pine bookcases on either side. Ben walked up to the chest-high spark screen and saw that it was welded from hefty iron bars and steel mesh. He grasped the top bar and pushed on it. The screen did not budge.

"This is quite a spark screen. I've never seen anything like it. It's tall and very strong." *Like a cage for a wild animal,* Ben thought. "There's a gate with a padlock. Why the lock?"

"I overbuild everything. I got the metal at the local landfill. I used it all. That's why it's so big. It does keep my grandkids away from the fire. I lock it up when they are here and the fire is going."

Ben looked at the fireplace wall, "Anything in the way outside on that end of the house? Water well? Septic tank? Drainage field?"

"It's all clear."

"What about property line setbacks, area and deed restrictions, Adirondack Park codes?"

"Clear, clear. Check the exterior. I think it should work."

"Then that sounds like the right spot. Let me take a quick look to see how it would tie in."

Ben went out on the porch and walked around to the end of the house, across a varied-colored slate path.

"How does it look?" Van Meer said, coming around the corner of the house and planting the black cane in the rocky turf.

"Hey, you shouldn't be out here."

"It's okay. This will get my mind cleared up. So what about the addition? Can it be done?"

"I don't see any problems. I assume you want it winterized?"

"Oh yes. I don't want any freezing pipes. This is my year-round home." Van Meer pointed at the cottage next door, slightly uphill from his. "My neighbor's cottage was not winterized when it was built, and it cost him more to do it later." He walked up the hill a few yards and stood next to Ben, both men looking uphill. "If we agreed on a price, would working over on this side of the lake be a problem for you? You could park your truck in Hague and come over by boat."

"Perhaps," Ben said.

"You could tie your boat up at my dock and live in my cottage while you work here and get some extra fishing in."

"That sounds inviting."

Ben heard a phone ring, and Van Meer turned down the hill, pointing over his shoulder. "That's my neighbor's phone."

It rang twice and stopped.

"Let's go back inside," Van Meer said. "I'd like to sit down."

"Are you okay?"

"Oh yes, just a little weak."

"You shouldn't have come outside."

Inside, Van Meer sat down in the rocker. Ben took the couch. Van Meer asked, "Were you trained as an architect?"

"Yes, I have a degree in architecture, but at my grandfather's suggestion, I went into the business of actually building my own designs."

"It sounds like you have a very smart grandfather."

"He was a good businessman."

"He has passed on?"

"No. He's still going strong."

"Did your wife help you in the business?"

"Yes, she did."

"I'm sure that everything will work out with you and your wife."

"My father permanently abandoned me and my mother when I was very young."

"I am sorry to hear that. But your wife and children have not permanently abandoned you."

"I know," Ben said.

"Why did your father abandon you?" Van Meer asked.

"He had other, greater passions than his family."

"How did he make a living? We Europeans are very interested in professions."

"He was an engineer."

"Like me," Van Meer said, pointing at the bookcase. "See those objects on the bookshelf?"

Ben glanced at two unidentifiable metal contraptions.

"I am a frustrated inventor," Van Meer said. "That thing on the left is a can opener that rolls up the lid into a tube, leaving no sharp edges. The other thing was supposed to be a remote-controlled location device to help you find lost items, like car keys or eyeglasses. So, that's what I like to do in my spare time—invent. How about you, Ben? What are your hobbies?"

"Fishing, boxing."

"Boxing? Where do you box?"

"A club."

"That's a very interesting hobby," Van Meer said, adding, "for an architect. I don't like anything where I can get physically hurt. My father was a very physical man. I was the opposite. How about your father, Ben, what was he like?"

"My memories of him are brief. And not very nice. I remember that he became mean when he drank too much."

"That is the curse of the drink. I'm only a social drinker, ja, ja. Except that my social life is like a vacuum, so I rarely drink. I like to be clearheaded all the time. That's the best route. Don't you agree?"

Ben nodded as he took a sip of the coffee.

"And your mother? Tell me about her," Van Meer said.

"My mother is dead. She was murdered."

"Murdered? My God, Ben. Such a sad life you've had. I hope they caught and punished the person who killed your mother."

"No, they didn't."

"And you lost contact with your father completely?"

"Yes. He may have been killed in the war."

"You don't know for sure? I'm astonished. Americans work very hard on finding missing soldiers."

"He wasn't American. He was a German soldier."

Van Meer was taken aback. "I assumed you were born in America."

"No, I was born in Germany."

"Where?" he asked eagerly.

"Dresden."

"I was in Dresden before the war. It was a beautiful city."

"Not after February 1945."

"I never understood why the Allies had to firebomb it. The Allies had us beat. Destroying Dresden was not necessary."

That's it. Ben just heard it. Van Meer was not Dutch. He just said, "The Allies had us beat." He said, "us," the Nazis.

"I lived in Dresden with my mother's family," Ben said.

"Did they survive the war?" Van Meer asked.

"They were Jews. What do you think?" Ben wished he had contained the snap in his reply.

"But you said your father was a German soldier. I don't understand."

"My mother was Jewish; my father was German. A true German of the Third Reich, right to the marrow," Ben said.

"How is that?"

"He was in the SS."

"In Hitler's time, that would make him a pretty good German. But with a Jewish wife, how did he ever get into the SS?"

"The SS didn't know about his wife and me."

Van Meer got up. "I need to get a drink of water."

"I'll get it for you."

"It's okay."

Van Meer went in the kitchen. Ben got up quickly and picked up the pill bottle, read the name of the drug Van Meer had taken, and then sat back down. Ben heard the faucet running, and then the phone rang, which Van Meer answered. "Hello. Ja. No, no. It's okay. Ja. Okay. No, no. No problem at all."

A few moments later, Van Meer came back in the living room with a glass of water. "That was my neighbor. He just got back. I left a message on his machine. He was concerned."

"The guy over here?" Ben pointed toward the end of the living room, where the new room might be added.

"Ja, ja. The guy with the freezing pipes."

Van Meer took out a pipe from an end table drawer. As he packed it with tobacco and lit it, Ben saw Van Meer's hand shaking.

"It smells smoky, like burning wood. What kind is it?"

"Virginia Hickory," Van Meer said. "It reminds me of—Holland, of home. My father smoked bacon. The wood smoke was similar." As Van Meer lit the pipe, he said, "My parents were both Dutch. But your situation must have been extremely sensitive because of your mother being Jewish and your father being in the SS. How did you know your father was in the SS?"

"I remember his uniform had the SS Death Head insignia."

"So you must have been older, not a small boy, when you last saw him?"

"Sixteen."

"Do you remember him?"

"I remember exactly what he looked like in 1944."

Van Meer glanced out at the lake framed by the picture window. "It was a terrible time. A disgraceful, shameful part of history. Many Germans still can't face it. The world is not letting them forget what they did. It was barbarian, ja, barbarian."

Ben shuddered at the way Van Meer said, "Barbarian, ja, barbarian." Those words awakened a clear memory. He saw a drunk Hans Kroner standing in a flung-open bedroom doorway of Baron Kroner's estate, shouting, "Barbarian, ja, barbarian."

Ben stood up and walked over to the window, then turned around and looked down at Van Meer. He had heard enough. He decided to do it now. "I need to know something about you, Mr. Van Meer."

"What is that?"

"I have a suspicion about you."

"Suspicion, Ben?" Van Meer seemed taken aback.

"I don't think your real name is Van Meer."

Van Meer smiled incredulously. "You don't. Who do you think I am, ja, who?"

"First, I don't think you had a real heart attack. Those are not nitroglycerin pills. The label says they are an extract of the cinchona bark. That's quinine. Pills for malaria. I think you pretended you had an attack to get me back here to find out who I was. You also have suspicions about me. Isn't that so?"

"I did have a heart problem. Yes, those are quinine pills. The nitro bottle is in the kitchen. I take the quinine for another complicated condition. Suspicions? What are you saying, Ben? What? I don't have to play games to find out who you are. I know who you are. You told me who you are. Did you not tell me the truth?"

"I think you're scared, Mr. Van Meer."

"Scared of what?"

"Scared of what I might do to you."

"Do what, Ben? I don't understand."

"I think you do."

"Please, Ben, explain, ja, explain. This is so sudden. I am shocked."

"Aren't you afraid I might turn you in?"

"Turn me in? To whom?"

"I think you know."

"Know what, Mr. Steinhardt? Please tell me. Know what?"

"Aren't you afraid of Nazi hunters? Aren't you afraid of being deported to stand trial in Israel or Germany? Aren't you? Didn't you get me back here because you thought I might be a Nazi hunter?"

"But, Ben, why would I think that? Ja, why? I was not a Nazi. I am from Holland, Ben. The Dutch hated the Nazis. Who do you think I am? And who are you, please tell me?"

"I think you are Hans Kroner."

Van Meer shook his head in disbelief and looked down at the floor. "Who? I have never heard of this Kroner. And what does it matter? I know who I am. Ben, you are out in left field, as they say in America. Ja, ja, in left field. Who was this Hans Kroner?"

"An SS killer."

"Ben, Ben, this is crazy. I am not this SS person you suspect me of being."

"Do you know a Manfred Aaron Kroner?"

"No. I never heard of him. Ja, never, never."

Van Meer placed his head in his hands and set both elbows down on his knees. "All this is crazy, Ben, ja, crazy. You're making me very upset."

"Your boat is named the *MANNY A*. Manny is a shortened version of Manfred, and A stands for Aaron."

"Manny stands for my daughter Amanda, and the A is for my deceased wife Audrey. I explained that to you this morning."

"You speak English with a German accent."

"Mr. Steinhardt, I am Dutch, not German. It is quite possible that the Germans and the Dutch might speak English with similar accents. You have everything wrong."

"You have a limp. Hans Kroner could have had a limp."

"I told you what happened to my leg, Ben." Van Meer stood up and pulled up his right trouser, exposing the artificial leg to the knee. His face was tense. "Your suspicions and accusations are upsetting me. I should ask you to leave."

"You should, but you won't. And I'll tell you why you won't."

"I don't need to know why. This is very upsetting. Getting acquainted with you was a mistake. I want you to leave my house."

"You know I'm telling the truth. There's one more thing, Mr. Van Meer."

"I have had enough of this. I insist you leave here now or I will call the police."

"One of Hans Kroner's favorite expressions was, 'Barbarian, ja, barbarian.' You just said those words exactly like Hans Kroner said on Christmas Eve in 1944 at Baron Kroner's, your father's estate in Germany."

Van Meer looked at Ben intensely. "Who are you?"

"The night you said those words is very clear to me. You must remember Helga, your mistress. Don't you remember that party with Martin Ulricht and your other SS friends, Dieter, Erwin? You must remember that night and what you did that night right in front of a wooden sailboat named the *MANNY A*. I'll never, ever forget it or forgive it, you murdering son of a bitch."

Chapter 14

In 1944, Manny's mother, Sarah Henkel, arrived at the Hitler Youth camp on Christmas Eve morning.

Exhausted and frightened, she sat at a table in the camp's dining hall. The young boys looked at her with dismay and suspicion. They suspected she was a Jew. She expected to be grabbed and arrested by the Gestapo or one of their cohorts at any moment. Despair circled her eyes and hollowed her cheeks; she looked broken and frayed. She had not eaten in days. Manny had last seen her horror-stricken face at the Swiss border, when Martin Ulricht had murdered her father, his grandpa Aaron Henkel. The beautiful velvet green dress she had made for Yom Kippur many years ago was ravaged and ripped by weeks of running and hiding. The atonement day outfit was now dirty, colorless, hanging apprehensively on her frail frame.

"You should not have come here," Manny said. "Commandant Stork hates me. My father has been the only visitor. According to the school records, my mother is dead and definitely not a Jew. Stork will call the Gestapo. Who did you tell them you were?"

"An aunt." Then her expression became dark and troubled. "No one knows you have a Jewish mother. No one knows that Hans Kroner has a Jewish wife and son. I've come to take you away, Ari," she said, coughing, crossing thin, pallid fingers on her chest.

"You have to eat something," he said. "You look very weak."

"I am defeated. What you see is defeat. But I will pull myself together to get you away from here."

She was the only Henkel who called him Ari. It wasn't even the shortened version of his middle name, Aaron. Ari was a name for a Palestinian Jew, an ancient name. She had started to call him that when he was a baby. At first, it was whispered when she laid him to sleep, but as he grew older, she used it regularly. He couldn't remember if she had ever called him Manny or Aaron. Never Manfred.

A student sentry suddenly arrived at the door. "There is no time." Manny grabbed his mother's arm. "Pretend you're sick. Let's go. Hurry."

He helped her get up, felt her body almost collapse on his arm. She was weak, but his strength waxed as hers waned. As they moved toward the door, he whispered, "Hold your hand on your stomach."

The student guard, Wolfgang Strasser, a football player and one of the few boys Manny got along with, barred the door.

"This is my aunt, Wolfgang," Manny said. "She's really sick. She had mashed potatoes at the Fat Goose. I have to take her to the toilet. She's about to throw up."

Wolfgang stepped aside. "I am sorry you are not feeling well. Please be hasty. Commandant Stork instructed me to not let you leave the dining hall."

"We'll be very quick," Manny said.

The bathroom was down the hall. Manny locked the door and ran for the window, opened it, and climbed out. He pulled his mother through the window headfirst. She summoned some covert hoard of stamina and pressed forward. They ran along the back of the building, around the end, across a driveway, along a line of beech trees. He told her to hide behind a huge tree along the main road leading out of the school grounds. Then, he hurried back across the road to the Administration Building.

At the back of the stone building was Stork's BMW motorcycle. A black leather coat, leather cap, and goggles were in the sidecar. Stork wanted people to think he was in the Gestapo, and so he dressed in black. Manny quickly put on the oversized coat and cap and pushed the motorcycle around to the gymnasium side of the building, where there were no doors or first floor windows. He jumped on, kick-started it, and drove off.

He pulled into the beech grove and stopped. He had to take off the cap and goggles before his mother would come around the trees. She climbed into the sidecar. "Crawl down as low as you can," he said, throwing the blanket over her.

Manny sped out of the campgrounds, zieg heiling a groundskeeper with the same exuberance and fervor as Stork.

An hour later, they pulled off to the side of the road.

Manny said, "Aunt Freda's is about an hour from here," Manny said. "We'll go there first. You can sit up now."

"Where did Ulricht take the rest of my family, Ari?" his mother asked as the wind blew hard against her face, making her squinting eyes run with black tears.

"I don't know," Manny said. "He left me at the youth camp and took them away in the truck. How did you know where to find me?"

"I called your aunt Freda, and she told me which Hitler Youth camp you were in."

As the motorcycle picked up speed, he realized the tears that were washing his mother's cheeks were not from the wind. "My poor, poor father," she said several times before her face fell into her brittle fingers.

Two hours later, while his shivering mother waited in the horse stable, Manny Kroner entered the back door of Freda Kroner's country manor. Because one of Freda's primary loves was food, Manny knew that the pantry would be well stocked. He walked quietly across the black and white tiled floor. As he was about to open the pantry, he saw the decorated Christmas tree in the entry foyer. The tree almost touched the ceiling. Manny was annoyed to see a silver swastika sitting on the top of the tree. He listened to the house. The brass pendulums of the large clock in the hallway swung steadily as the painting of the Fuehrer stood watch like a sentry or a witness to prevent the removal of the swastika from the zenith of the spruce.

Manny opened the door to the pantry. The room smelled of smoked meat. Out in the cold stable, his mother was hungry, cold, and sick. He wished he could bring her into the heated house, to food and a warm bed. But she had warned him not to wake Freda Kroner, his father's sister. Manny had argued with his mother, had said Freda would be kind and hospitable to them and wouldn't turn them into the Gestapo. But she had insisted that he get some bread, perhaps some smoked fish or cheese, anything to sustain them on their journey. The motorcycle was hidden in the woods along the road. He needed petrol. Maybe he would find some in one of the estate's garages or siphon it from one of the Mercedes sedans.

Manny picked up one of the brown beer bottles lined up on the shelf, opened it, and took a swig. He filled his backpack with links of landyaeger, smoked ham and fish, cheese, and a loaf of black bread. Out of a ceramic jar, he took several pickles. Out of a wooden barrel, he grabbed some pears. As he swung the backpack around, the light in the kitchen snapped on. Manny slid his backpack under a shelf and snatched up the beer bottle. As he took a swig, Freda Kroner entered the pantry, holding a broom.

"Manfred, what are you doing here?"

Freda rolled in like a puffed-up cumulus cloud. She was expansive and substantial, but very nimble. She had knockwurst lips, crimson cheeks, and the cloudy eyes of a shoat. She smothered Manny against her ashen robe, smelling of cinnamon, chocolate, and smoked bacon.

Manny loved Freda, but did not know if he could trust her at this time. Everyone was frightened of the Gestapo. And if Freda had to lie to protect his mother, he didn't think she could do it.

"I was hungry," Manny said. "I didn't want to wake you. I was going to eat something and then go to sleep upstairs."

"Your father will be so glad to see you. You shouldn't be drinking beer at your age."

"Is my father here?"

"No." She released him. "Hans called to say he was coming. He will arrive tomorrow morning. He is very upset that you ran away from the youth camp and stole the commandant's motorcycle. I tried to calm him down. The Gestapo has been looking for you. Where have you been all this time? And for God's sake, where is your poor mother? She called me here a few days ago. I told her where you were. I am afraid for her life."

Manny took a sip of beer. "She visited me at the camp then took the train south to Munchen. I convinced her to go back to Switzerland. She has all the necessary papers to get in. Where have I been? Right now, I am being a good German." He raised the beer and pulled a landyaeger off a hook. "Good Germans drink beer and eat sausage and visit their aunts."

Freda Kroner smiled. "Always quick with the words, Manfred. That's what I like about you. You are a very smart boy."

"That's from the Jewish side."

"I am glad your mother went back to Switzerland to be with her family. Hans said all the Henkels are now in Switzerland."

"Not my grandfather Aaron. I saw Ulricht shoot him. And Ulricht took all the other Henkels away. Taken back into Germany, not left in Switzerland. Ulricht lied to my father."

"Ulricht is evil," Freda said. "I pray everyday that Hans parts company from him."

Manny took a swallow of beer.

"You're starving. I will make you a sandwich. Come, come. And what are all these cuts on your face? Don't tell me you were fighting again."

"I have to fight. The lunatics attack me."

"Why? I don't understand fighting."

"I like beating up the Nazi boys. I want them to know I can take care of myself. They're all a bunch of bullies. They talk tough, but they don't fight. They fight only as a pack. I got this cut from the biggest kid in the school. But I laid him out flat right after that. I hate that schmuck Klaus."

"Manny, I don't want you to use those words in my home."

"Sorry, Aunt Freda. Don't worry. I have never told anyone at the school the truth about my mother. No one there knows she's a Jew."

They went into the kitchen. While cutting the dark bread and spreading the tea wurst, Freda asked, "Why did you run away from the camp?"

"I left the camp to join the Wehrmacht."

"Manny, you are much too young for the army."

"I'm not too young. I'm sixteen, and I know I can fight. Besides, the Volkssturm Program is taking all males between fifteen and sixty."

"Fifteen is too young for war and sixty is too old."

Manny ate two sandwiches and drank the strong lager. Freda had a sandwich and a glass of milk. "Now, let's go to sleep. It's almost midnight. And don't tell Hans that I let you drink beer."

"Can I sleep in the living room by the coal stove?" Manny asked. "I can see the Christmas tree from there."

"Do you see what Hans put on top of the tree? He said that the star is inappropriate in these times."

"Why?"

"Well, you know...."

"The Star of Bethlehem stands for Christmas."

"I know. You're right, Manny."

"If this was my house, I'd put up the star."

"Hans is very political, and you're too young to fight the Russians. Hans doesn't like the star because it's painted on American military vehicles."

"You're right about my father and wrong about me."

Freda got Manny some blankets out of a closet. "Your father always brings friends, I keep the blankets and pillows handy for the men to sleep down here." As she tucked Manny in, she said, "I am so happy you came here. It will be a nice Christmas after all."

When she was upstairs and sleeping, Manny got up took three blankets and a pillow, got his backpack, and went out to the stable. His mother was shivering in one corner.

Chapter 15

In the stable, Manny led his feverish mother to a dark corner, where he lifted off the canvas cover from a small sailboat. She muttered, "Is this the *MANNY A?*"

"Yes," he said.

"I know your father gave you this boat for your tenth birthday. He taught you to sail on the Elbe."

He helped her into the boat and into the cuddy, where it was somewhat protected from the bitter cold. To make room, he had to move several boxes marked OFFICIAL DOCUMENTS OF THE THIRD REICH. He lit a candle and waxed it to a small plate.

Manny removed her worn shoes and socks and wrapped her feet in a blanket. She wore a wool dress with a thin sweater. He blanketed her and gave her bread and ham and beer. "I'm going to try and find better shoes or boots for you and a sweater and a hat and food."

She asked. "Does Freda know anything about my family?"

Manny said. "Hans told Freda they were in Switzerland."

"Good. Hans must have told Ulricht to take them back."

"I hate my father and Martin Ulricht. I will kill Ulricht for what he did."

She took his hand. "Your grandfather Aaron was very proud of you. He said that you would go far in the world. He said you were the bravest boy he has ever known. Do you remember that night when he hadn't come home and you went looking for him? We waited and waited. Then finally you returned. Your grandpa said that he had been surrounded by three or four Nazi youths and you had stepped between them and your grandfather. He said you punched the biggest one, the leader of the group, right in the mouth and knocked a tooth out and the others immediately backed off. Your grandpa Aaron said that the rest of the boys sensed you were too ferocious for them and ran off. He said the boys called you, 'Crazy Jew. Crazy Jew.' He said you showed no fear of them and that's why you scared them off and saved him from a beating."

"The whole trick with bullies is not to show them you are afraid of them," Manny said. "It throws them off guard. And when they're off guard, you just let them have it as fast and hard as you know how. That's what I'm going to do to Martin Ulricht for killing Grandpa."

"No, no, Ari. Please don't." His mother reached out to him and took him in her arms. "You are a very brave boy, Ari, not a murderer. Stay away from Ulricht. God will take care of him for killing my dear father."

They looked at each other and were speechless for a long moment as they remembered Ulricht's murderous act at the Swiss border.

Chapter 16

Martin Ulricht had handed Manny's mother over to Swiss authorities. Manny saw her being held back by a tall man and a woman in a white coat. He saw Ulricht strutting back to the truck, lighting a cigarette.

Grandpa Aaron said to Ulricht, "We were all supposed to go to Switzerland. That's what my son-in-law, Hans Kroner promised."

"Hans Kroner is not here now. I have made a few alterations to his plans," Ulricht replied.

"Let Manfred go with his mother. He's still a boy. Only sixteen." Grandpa Aaron pleaded.

"Manfred is going back to the Hitler Jugend Camp. That's what his father wants."

Ulricht got in the cab. The truck engine started up. Grandpa Aaron threw his body onto the SS guard sitting on the bench at the opening of the truck. "Run, Manfred!"

Manny jumped out of the truck and started for the border, where his mother still waited. Ulricht got out and fired in the air. "Stop him. Stop him, don't shoot him. Bring him back alive."

The German border guards raised their rifles. Manny leapt into the ditch along the road, scrambled up the hillside into the rocks, then stopped and looked down.

Ulricht held the pistol to Grandpa Aaron's head. "Come down, Manfred, or I'll shoot your grandfather."

Manny came down out of the rocks.

The SS guard pushed Manny into the truck.

"Not you," Ulricht said to Grandpa Aaron. He marched Aaron over to the ditch and shot him in the back of the head.

Manfred leapt out of the truck and landed on Ulricht's back, knocking him down, digging his fingers into Ulricht's eyes. Then he was pulled away and flung into the back of the truck.

Chapter 17

Manny looked into his mother's distraught exhausted face and knew he had to get her to a safe warm place. The thought of his father returning to the Kroner estate the next day forced him to his feet. He guessed Ulricht would be with him. When wasn't he? They were always together. They shadowed each other. He didn't tell his mother that Hans Kroner was coming to the house. She was sick and needed to rest.

"We can't stay here, Ari," she said. "Maybe we should leave this instant. I feel better already."

"It's midnight. Let's rest until two. I have to find fuel for the motorcycle."

As Manny left, the stallion, Hector, milled around fitfully. He found several military cans of gasoline in one of the garages and carried one out to the woods where he had hidden the motorcycle. He filled the tank and stuck the rest of the can in the sidecar. It was a clear, cold night. He started the motorcycle, let it run for a few seconds, turned it off, and threw a tarp over it to protect it if it snowed. He thought about getting his mother now and leaving and forgetting about Ulricht. They could drive through the night, get away before Ulricht before and his father arrived, but the thought of Ulricht kept him from leaving. He wanted to avenge his grandfather's cold-blooded murder. He didn't know how, but he was going to kill Ulricht.

When he got back in the house, he went in the closet where Aunt Freda kept the Christmas decorations and found a silver star. He got a chair and replaced the swastika on the Christmas tree.

From an upstairs guest room, he got an alarm clock. He wound the clock and set the alarm for 3:00 a.m., then lay back on the couch and pulled the blankets over him. He had decided that at 3:00 a.m., he would leave. He would take his mother to safety. To Switzerland.

As he lay under the covers, he could see that the star on top of the tree had captured and reflected some hidden light in the house that Manny could not see.

Chapter 18

The first breath of morning ejected from the sloppy mouth of Rumpel,
Hans Kroner's German shepherd. Manny opened his eyes to Rumpel's red
tongue and rapid breathing. He sat up. The alarm had not gone off. Several
men were sleeping on the floor. Standing in the doorway in front of the
Christmas tree was his father, Hans Kroner. He wore a black uniform with
the death head on the hat, Standartenfuhrer oak leaves on the collar, and a
death head armband. Manny saw that the swastika was back on the treetop.
His father's steely eyes bored into Manny. The expression was familiar.
His father motioned to him with his jutting chin. Manny swung his legs to
the floor and reached for his pants.

"You won't need those," his father said.

Barefoot, in his underwear, Manny followed his father out to the stable.
Rumpel trailed behind them, sniffing the frozen ground. Inside the barn,
Hans Kroner yanked off his black belt and grabbed Manny by the ear. He
forced him down over a wheelbarrow and began to pelt him across the
bottom.

"Tomorrow I will take you back to the camp," Kroner said. "This is
your punishment for running away. Now, tell me where your mother is."

"In Switzerland, where Ulricht left her."

Kroner struck. "Smartass. Where is your mother? She is in danger."

"Yeah, from you and Ulricht."

Kroner hit him again and said, "Alone, she will never survive. You can't help her. Only I can protect her. Where is she? I will get her to Switzerland. She was with you when you ran away from the camp. Where did she go?"

"She took the train to Munchen."

"Don't lie to me. The Gestapo was at the station. They would have picked her up."

"There's a river outside the town with an old bridge. All the trains slow down as they cross the bridge. She got on the slow-moving train outside of town, beyond the bridge. I took her there. I helped her get on the train."

"Why didn't you go with her?"

"I didn't have the proper papers to get into Switzerland."

"She doesn't either. You're lying. Where is Stork's motorcycle?"

"It ran out of gas four or five kilometers from here. I walked here."

"You're lying."

Manny sprang up from the wheelbarrow. "I'm not going back to that sissy camp. There's something else I'd rather do."

"What's that?"

"I want to join the Wehrmacht."

"The Wehrmacht?" Kroner laughed. "The Wehrmacht is for men."

"Is that why you and Ulricht aren't in it?"

The slap was sudden and hard.

Manny flinched, but didn't move his hand to his cheek. He looked around as if there were a buzzing mosquito nearby. "Your slap has no sting. Now I see why we're losing the war."

"Tough guy, eh?" Kroner smiled. "Well, well. That's commendable. But you're too young to be fighting Russians, Manfred. You're going back to the Hitler Juegen camp. When you stop doing things that land you ass end up in a wheelbarrow, you will be ready for the Wehrmacht."

"Then I want to be in the Waffen SS," Manny lied. "You can get me in. Isn't the Waffen SS also fighting the Russians?"

"Out of the question. The SS is not for children, and definitely not for my son. What would your mother think and say if she knew you were in the SS?"

"Why did you let Ulricht kill my grandpa Aaron?"

"What?"

"Ulricht shot him in front of his family."

"I didn't know. I swear it. Where did it happen? Why?" Kroner asked, appearing genuinely stunned. "Tell me everything."

After Manny described the events at the Swiss border, Kroner rushed out of the stable.

Chapter 19

Rumpel was near the *MANNY A.* with his paws on the gunnel, sniffing the canvas cover. His mother had probably heard everything. He was glad he hadn't yelled out in pain. Rumpel started to bark.

Manny found a stick of wood and said, "Come on boy, let's go out, come on boy, let's go play." As soon as he had the dog outside, Manny threw the stick away from the barn. Rumpel ran after it and brought it back. He led Rumpel to the edge of the woods and said, "Go hunt, boy. Go hunt."

Rumpel sniffed the ground and started to follow a rabbit's tracks. Manny ran back inside the stable, closed the door, behind him and climbed into the *Manny A.* In the cuddy, his mother was sitting up, holding her face in her hands. "I heard Hans. I heard him."

"Go back to sleep," Manny said. "It's safe to sleep. We'll leave as soon as I get a chance."

She fell back and pulled the blanket over her.

As Manny walked back to the house, Rumpel caught up with him by the kitchen door. Manny pulled the stick out of the dog's mouth and threw it again.

In the living room, the men were awake, getting dressed. They all greeted Manny warmly. Manny knew all of them. There was Martin, Erwin, and Dieter. He hated all three. Especially Martin Ulricht.

Martin said, "Manfred, I know you have great skills as a pugilist." He came closer to Manny and feigned a few punches. "In my youth, I too was a boxer. Come and show me how you block a punch."

Manny shook his head as he picked up his socks and pants. "I don't think so. Hitting Germans got me into trouble."

Dieter laughed and sat up. "Martin is very fast. Five marks says you can't lay a hand on him."

"Ten says he can," Erwin said. "I've heard about Manfred's speed and power."

Martin feigned a few more punches.

Manny put on his pants and shoes. Martin grabbed him by the shoulder. Manny swung his right arm around and knocked his grip loose. Then he unleashed three quick punches to Martin's stomach, one of them into the solar plexus. Martin bent over, gasping for air. Manny looked down and wanted to pull the Luger out of the holster belted around Martin Ulricht. Just pull it out and put a bullet in his head, the same as Ulricht had to his grandfather.

Erwin laughed. "Pay up. Now you see why they call him Little Max Schmeling."

Martin was having a hard time regaining air. Manny ran out of the room and up the stairs just as Kroner entered and said, "Martin, I need to speak to you privately."

In the main bathroom cabinet, Manny found an aspirin bottle. He shook out a handful and put the tablets in his pants pocket. He walked down the stairs. He heard his father and Ulricht arguing in the kitchen. He moved in closer and listened.

Ulricht said, "All of your wife's family are back in Switzerland. I just gave them a little tour of the Fatherland, to one of the relocation centers. Just to show them that if they didn't behave, they'd wind up in one. They're all in Zurich now, taking out the money they had hoarded away in the Swiss banks."

Kroner looked down at the floor.

"Enough now, Hans," Ulricht said. "No more discussion of this business with the Henkels. I know you understand."

Manny heard the door slam. Ulricht had walked out and his father had said absolutely nothing about Ulricht killing Aaron Henkel. Nothing.

At that moment, Freda came into the kitchen and Kroner attacked her immediately. "The silver swastika ornament on the Yule tree was given to me by Reichsfuhrer Himmler. It's pure silver. Why did you remove it?"

Freda said, "I did it because I don't think it belongs on a Christmas tree."

"Correction, Freda. That is a Yule tree. We are not celebrating the birth of a Jew; we are celebrating the winter solstice. What am I going to do with you? Luckily, I was able to remove the star before my men saw it. The Kroner household is National Socialist. I order you not to stray from that."

"This was a Lutheran house before Hitler," Freda said.

"And Luther was no lover of the Jews," Kroner said. "I am a man of the Reich, a man of nature, a barbarian. I celebrate the winter solstice, not the birth of a Jew. So, Freda, I am having a small party tonight for the men who are fighting for the Fatherland."

Freda didn't hide her displeasure. "I don't want those women here. I thought we had an agreement. I don't want the parlor of our parents' home turned into a brothel. Baron and Baroness Kroner would not approve of this."

"Freda, this is war," Hans Kroner said, "I want to do this for my men. We're going back to fighting Russians shortly. A small farewell party is the least I can do. You are mistaken, Baron Kroner probably did the very same thing during the Great War."

"But Hans, not that kind of party, not on Christmas Eve, not in our family's ancestral home. For generations, the birth of Jesus was celebrated here. Alcohol and loose women were never allowed. Never. Not in your mother's house."

"National Socialism does not regard Jesus the Jew as one deserving reverence. The Fuehrer has ordered all Semitic history out of our lives. Jesus is Semite number one."

"Perhaps for you this is a heathen time, but not for me. That is not what our parents taught us, Hans, what the Lutheran Church taught us. We were taught to love and believe in Christ. I will not stay here tonight. Manny and I will go to my friend Hilda's house."

"For you, that will be better. But Manny will stay with me. I don't want him out of my sight before I bring him back to the youth camp. We will be gone by noon tomorrow. Everything will be left clean and orderly."

"I don't want to see a trace of anything."

"Don't worry, Freda. And by the way, I think you should read Martin Luther's views on the Jews."

Manny walked into the kitchen.

"Good morning, Manny," Aunt Freda said. "Your father has come."

"We have already seen each other," Hans Kroner said.

"I'll make you pancakes. Sit down, Manny."

Ulricht entered, rubbing his palms from the cold.

"Do you know how to make potato blintzes?" Manny asked. He remained standing.

"Of course. I'll make them for you. It will take a little longer."

"Blintzes are permitted in the Kroner household?" Ulricht said. "Blintzes are not German cuisine, Freda. Aren't we Germans?"

"That's ridiculous," Freda said. "Blintzes have always been eaten in Germany."

"Not by good and proper Germans. Only Jews eat blintzes. Very few now, Freda, and fewer by the hour. Hans, are you going to let your sister stimulate your son with the Yiddish blintz? His consuming of blintzes will detract from our great success in reducing the blintz-consuming culture."

Hans agreed. "Ja, ja, Freda, no blintzes. Martin is correct."

Manny hated his father at this moment more than he ever had before. Hans Kroner was a subordinate; Ulricht was in charge.

Manny saw the strange symbol of rings and death heads on the armband of his father's uniform. Hans Kroner was sucking in black, boiling-hot coffee through tightly pursed lips. Manny hated the sibilant sound and the inflexible look on his father's face. He saw the black Luger strapped to his father's belt. Hans saw him looking at it. "Come, Manfred. It's time you learned to shoot like a Kroner. Baron Kroner was a crack shot." Hans grabbed a towel. "Freda, I need some tacks."

Freda rummaged through a drawer and gave Hans a handful of thumbtacks. "He's too young to be shooting."

Hans tacked up the white towel on the barn and walked back across the yard. He explained how the pistol worked and said, "Think of the target as a Russian. Ja, ja, make it a Russian. At least they know enough to run and show us their backside."

Martin Ulricht stuck his head out of the kitchen door. "Not like the Jews, eh, Hans? They don't even run, do they?" He drew back and slammed the door.

Manny and Kroner faced the barn. Hans aimed and took the first shot. Then he gave the gun to Manny. "Hold it steady. Remember, the towel is an enemy of the Reich."

Manny was afraid that a ricocheting bullet could hit his mother in the *MANNY A.* "Can't we tack the towel to that dead tree next to the barn? It will look more like a retreating Russian."

Freda flung open the kitchen door. "Hans, I can't believe you are shooting holes in your father's stable."

Hans moved the towel to the dead tree.

Manny fired. The gun almost flew out of his hand.

"Hold it tighter. There's recoil. Use both hands."

Manny fired again and again.

When the gun was empty, they walked over to the target. Manny had hit the towel once.

As they walked back toward the house, Manny asked his father about the rings and death heads on the armband.

As Kroner reloaded the Luger, he said, "That's top secret. All I can say is we do very special work for Reichsfuhrer Himmler."

"What do you do?"

"Ensure that the Fatherland and its conquered lands are properly prepared. No more questions about work, Manfred. Now, I want you to learn how to shoot."

Prepared for what? Manny wondered. Then he asked, "Have you killed Jews?"

"Never, not ever, not once," Kroner said. "And never believe what Martin tells you."

Hans showed Manny where the safety was located. He left Manny in the yard with two dozen cartridges. While he practiced shooting, Manny saw Rumpel sniffing around the perimeter of the barn. When Manny regarded the towel as Martin Ulricht, his aim improved. The last ten slugs hit the towel perfectly. He reloaded the gun, chambered one round and entered the house.

He opened the door, holding the Luger waist high. Ulricht's hand shot out from behind the door and grabbed the pistol. "No guns in the kitchen, little soldier."

Manny sat down to have a bowl of cream of wheat and brown sugar.

Ulricht said he couldn't stomach any kind of porridge and had brought his own breakfast, smoked salmon. As Ulricht sliced off a shaving of pink salmon meat and laid it on his tongue, Manny said, "My Grandfather Aaron also ate lachs for breakfast. He said it was an old family custom. A Jewish custom."

The other SS men laughed and ribbed Ulricht for indulging in a Jewish breakfast.

"Eat the blintzes," Manny said. "Blintzes go well with lachs."

Ulricht glared at Manny and pushed the plate of salmon away.

Watching Ulricht eat made Manny sick. He got up and went outside to play with Rumpel, who was barking near the barn door.

Manny found the stick in the yard and tossed it at Rumpel. He led Rumpel around to the back of the property, to the fence behind the thick fir trees where he lifted up the loose wire. Manny liked Rumpel, but he didn't want him snooping around the barn and revealing his mother's hiding place. Rumpel wiggled through, sniffed the frozen ground, and loped off into the woods. The surrounding, fenced-in private forest was vast and filled with game. Being a natural hunter, Rumpel would be gone a long time.

Manny returned to the barn and climbed into the *MANNY A*. His mother was awake, eating bread. He gave her the aspirin and felt her head. She was feverish and sweating and said that they had to leave as soon as it was dark. After taking the pills, she lay down.

She said, "I looked in those boxes and there are numerous documents and ledger style books with rows of columns and dates and numbers from places like Sobibor and Auschwitz. Some of the documents are about something called the 'Final Solution of the Jewish Question.'"

Manny covered her and went back to the house.

He would return after dark, and they would escape.

Chapter 20

In the driveway at the front of the house, Freda Kroner said goodbye to Manny and told him not to run away from the youth camp again. Manny watched her drive off as another car pulled into the driveway.

Four giggling women got out of a black Mercedes. Manny had seen one of them before. He knew what kind of women they were. The one he knew called him over. "Manfred, come here."

She was Helga, his father's girlfriend. She kissed Manny on the cheek, leaving a red smear. Helga was dark-haired and wore a fur coat. The five jewels in her black beret sparkled in the sunlight. She hugged him close to her silky, cool sable and said to the other women, "This is Manny, Hans Kroner's son. Isn't he a handsome boy? An untamed youth, a handful, so Hans has told me."

The women smiled and said it was a pleasure to meet him.

Manny liked the way Helga had pulled him close to her and held him against the soft, perfumed fur.

The one they called Baanhoff Brigitta asked, "Is it true that at the youth camp, the girls are very free?"

Manny smiled. "Some of them."

"Have you had some ooh la la with them?"

"I'm a healthy German boy. What do you think?"

"Manny, I'm surprised," Helga said. "I didn't think you were interested in girls."

As he pulled away from her, he said, "What do you think I am? Of course I like girls. The more the better." He walked off, leaving the women laughing.

Chapter 21

Kroner's men and the "fille de jois," as Ulricht referred to the four women originally from Hamburg's Reeperbahn, had been drinking, eating, dancing, and singing for several hours. Outside, a hoary cold rubbed against the stone mansion.

Manny checked on his mother at one point. He brought out a bottle of soda water, some apples, and chocolates. The backpack was filled with food and packed into the motorcycle's sidecar. She was sound asleep. For a moment, he listened to her breathing. He would have to get her up in a few hours. Before dawn, they would have to make their escape. On the way back to the house, Rumpel ran up to him.

When Manny walked into the kitchen, he walked in on his father kissing Helga. His father's hand was under Helga's skirt; in the other hand was a glass of schnapps. Manny saw that his father was drunk. He was sickened by his father's flushed face, his narrowed, reddened eyes. He knew the festering rage that could erupt at any second, that it was a word or a look removed.

Kroner shouted into the parlor, "Martin, come in here."

Ulricht, pulling up his pants and wearing no shirt, ran in.

"Take Manfred upstairs and lock him in the third-floor bedroom. The small one on the end of the house."

Then Kroner grabbed Helga by the arm and said, "It is time my son learned about the birds and the bees."

"I think he knows," Helga said. "Manfred told me all about the girls at the Hitler Youth camp."

"Don't believe him. Manfred is very good at twisting the truth. I want you to teach him. Manfred, this is my Yule present to you." He pushed Helga toward him. "Helga will make a German out of you. You already know how to fight and shoot. Now, you must learn how to make love. Ja, ja, make love."

Helga said, "But Hans, it is not right. I am old enough to be his mother."

Hans pushed her away. "Take him upstairs, Martin. I will speak with Helga."

Ulricht pushed Manny out of the kitchen. Manny heard Helga yell out, and suspected Kroner had struck her.

From the downstairs parlor came laughter. A woman sang "Lili Marlene" on the phonograph. Ulricht locked the third-floor bedroom door. There was no way out, not even through the window Manny had opened; the frozen ground was thirty feet below. There was a blanket and a sheet on the bed. Tying them together would still place him twenty feet above the hard ground. He could see the stable where his mother was hiding in the *MANNY A.*, hopefully sleeping, fighting off her fever, waiting for him to come and take her to safety, to Switzerland. He guessed it was around one in the morning. There was still time to get away.

He heard the stamping of feet ascending the stairs. He heard the key inserted, the click of the box lock opening, and the door swinging open.

In a drunken state, Kroner stumbled in, dragging Helga by the arm. He pulled her around in front of Manny and pushed her toward him. "Here is my Yule present to you. She will make a barbarian, ja, a barbarian of you."

Helga turned to Kroner and whispered something Manny could not hear. Kroner slapped her across the face, turned, and marched out of the room, slamming the door shut. Manny saw Helga's shoulders slump while she held one hand to her cheek. Manny didn't hear the turn of the key or the footfalls descending the stairs.

Helga turned. "This is an impossible moment. You are just a boy."

Manny put his index finger across his mouth and tiptoed towards the door and listened. He put his ear to the door and motioned that Kroner was out there listening.

Helga raised her voice, acted out. "It will be my pleasure to make you a barbarian."

Awkwardly, they exchanged words then Helga whispered, "We'll just pretend we did it."

The door flew open and Kroner stood glaring in the opening.

"Do you want me to stand here and watch my son receive his Yule gift?"

Helga glanced at Manny. "No. Please leave, Hans. I'll do it."

After the door closed and was locked, Kroner descended the stairs.

Helga turned off the lights and they undressed, and soon were naked under the blankets.

"I hated him before he hit you," Manny said. "I hate him now. I'll hate him for the rest of my life."

"Don't think about him now." Helga brushed his hair back. "We have almost the same color brown hair. Your eyes are a darker blue than your father's, and you have long lashes."

"The darkness comes from my mother."

"You are a handsome young man."

Helga's arm encircled him and pulled him closer. The feel of her breasts against his body excited him. He felt her sweet warmth. She giggled. "I can feel you. Is it true?" She picked up the blanket and glanced down. "It is true. Your little barbarian is a fully grown Hun."

She took his face in her hands. "If you don't want to do this, it is all right too."

Not knowing what to say, Manny remained silent.

"We could just as well do what we're supposed to do, as long as you agree," Helga said. "It would be my great pleasure, even though the first time should be with your bride. But these are such terrible times and there are so many girls who will never be brides and too many boys who will never be grooms. In this unpredictable time, this is an exceptional moment. I don't think that it will be wrong. What do you think?"

He was abandoned in sweet, unknown territory, in a zone of rising excitement. He didn't know what to do, but she saw—or sensed—the confusion of his feelings and chose the most bewildering, innocence, and guided him away from it forever.

Chapter 22

Rumpel's bark woke him. Helga was gone from the bed and from the room. Manny sprang up and got dressed and opened the window. Bitter, cold air rushed into the room. A blue mist hugged the ground.

He heard gunshots from the direction of the stable, from inside the stable. Manny bounded down the stairs, full of blame and reprehension.

He rushed across the yard toward the open door of the stable. He froze in the doorway when he saw his father holding a black Luger in his hand stooping next to the body of his mother, prone on the plank floor. Kroner looked stricken. He looked up at Manny and said, "She is dead. Your mother is dead."

There was a pile of garden tools stacked in the corner by the door. Manny seized an ax, ran toward Kroner and swung it at him. Kroner dodged. The heavy head of the tool thudded into the plank floor. Kroner screamed and grabbed his foot. Instantly, the blood started to seep out between Kroner's fingers onto his black boot. Manny tried to lift the handle of the ax, but it was embedded deep into the wood floor with a tip of the black boot cut off. Kroner screamed in pain.

Manny kneeled down beside his motionless mother, saw her blood on the floor and on her green dress. He took her hand, felt her head, hoped she would open her eyes. He put his ear to her chest, did not hear a heartbeat, looked into her cold face, wanted her cracked blue lips to whisper, "Ari."

Manny let go of her hand. The cameo broach of Aphrodite fell on the floor. He picked it up and stuck it in his pocket. Manny snatched up Kroner's Luger and aimed it at him. "Why? Why did you kill her?"

With pain wracking his face, his bloody hand cupping the tip of his black boot, Kroner sat on the floor. "I didn't do it. I didn't. I found her like that."

Then Manny felt something hard press against the back of his head and heard the commanding voice of Martin Ulricht. "Drop the pistol, little soldier."

Manny swung the Luger around. Ulricht's foot kicked the gun out of his hand. Manny drove his fist into Ulricht's groin. Ulricht doubled over as his own Luger fell out of his hand. Manny jumped to his feet, kicked Ulricht's gun across the plank floor, and dove for Kroner's. He picked the gun up and turned to Ulricht, who was gasping and holding his groin. Manny fired point blank at him. Click. Nothing. Misfired, or no load in the chamber. Manny pulled back the lever, and a shell ejected.

Still breathless and on his knees, Ulricht struggled for cover behind a stall. Manny fired again, but the gun only clicked. It was misfiring. He pulled the trigger again. Click. Empty. He threw the Luger down and looked for Ulricht's gun as Erwin and Dieter ran into the stable. Manny pushed past them and ran.

Chapter 23

"I want you to leave my house now," Van Meer said.

Ben clenched his fists to control himself and moved up to Van Meer. "On Christmas Eve 1944, you shot and killed Sarah Henkel in Baron Kroner's stable next to a small sailboat named the *Manny A*. I saw you standing over her with a Luger in your hand. Sarah Henkel was my mother. You killed my mother, you Nazi son of a bitch."

Van Meer grabbed his head and cradled it with both hands. "I never—I didn't—" He glanced at Ben uneasily, tentatively. His lower lip quivered. "Don't accuse me of that. You are wrong about that. Yes, I am Hans Kroner, you are right about that, but I did not kill your mother, my wife, Sarah Henkel. Who are you? What do you know about me? I insist you tell me."

"I am Manfred Aaron Kroner, your son."

"But you can't be. Manfred was killed during the war. You are a pretender. One of the Nazi hunters pretending you are Manfred. I can't believe this. My God, my God."

"You murdered my mother, you son of a bitch. And now you're going to pay for it."

Chapter 24

Ben released the grip on Kroner's bunched-up sweater and pushed him back down on the couch. Ben could not dislodge himself from the coiled, menacing stance over the man he saw murder his mother in cold blood.

An ashen Kroner, divided by shadow and sunlight, sat as if he were straddling a cryptic terminator between life and death. He glanced vigilantly at the afternoon sunlight streaming through the picture window. He pressed one hand to his chest, while he reached over with his other to an end table for a glass of water. Kroner's shoulders slumped and his voice was fragile. "If you are really Manfred, it is terrible that all of your life, you have believed that I murdered your mother. I am very sorry for what you have felt in losing her and thinking of me as a murderer, her murderer. I understand your hatred and anger toward me. But your feelings are baseless because of one simple fact, Manfred. I did not kill her. How could I have? She is not dead."

"Not dead? You were standing over her with a gun in your hand. You said, 'She is dead, your mother is dead.' What are you talking about?"

"The gun was in my hand, yes, and I did say she was dead because that is what I thought at that moment. Please be calm, Manfred. I can explain everything. I am so happy you are alive. Now you will hear and know the truth. Your mother is not dead. Please, sit down."

Knotted up, battling disbelief and a furious impulse to strike Kroner, Ben remained standing. "Go ahead. Explain it."

"To you, it certainly must have looked like I had killed her," Kroner said. He took a sip of water. "Do you remember Rumpel, our dog? Yes? His barking woke me. It was about five in the morning and still dark. I always rise early. As I was dressing, I heard shots coming from outside. I grabbed my pistol and shouted for the others to wake up. On my way to the stable, I thought maybe old Rumpel had cornered a thief or an enemy agent who had parachuted behind our lines to commit acts of sabotage or gather intelligence. That kind of activity was going on.

"With a drawn gun, I entered the stable and switched on the lights. Rumpel was sniffing a body lying on the floor near the *Manny A*. I leaned down next to the body partially wrapped in a blanket and was shocked to see that it was my own dear wife, Sarah. She had been shot. She wasn't breathing. I felt no pulse. I believed she was dead. It all happened so fast. Next, you ran in. I looked at you, and that's when I said, 'She is dead.' You must have thought I had done it. That is why you attacked me with the ax. I tried to get out of the way when you swung it. You missed my head, but severed two of my toes. Then, Martin Ulricht ran in and tried to detain you, but you ran off. Martin took me to a military hospital for medical treatment for my severed toes.

"An hour after I arrived at the hospital, Martin informed me that he had called Freda back, and she had told him that the doctor had pronounced my wife dead. I instructed Martin to call my sister to have your mother's body buried in the Kroner family plot at the estate. As her Jewish religion deemed it, she had to be buried before sundown of the day following her death. I could not go to the funeral because a blood infection had set in, and I was very, very sick. A few days later, Martin told me that the Gestapo had caught a British agent who confessed to killing a woman in the Kroner stable." Kroner paused to sip water.

"Then why do you say she is alive?" Ben asked.

"Wait," Kroner said, sitting up. "In 1975, I was living in America with my wife Audrey and daughter Amanda. For many years, I wanted to find out what happened to my sister Freda, but I was unable to do this because I was listed as a Nazi war criminal. Writing to my sister at the old Kroner estate with a return address or returning there was not possible.

"However, at that time, a high official in the East German government, for the right price, could get one safely in and out of East Germany. I trusted this official because he had once served in the SS. After many months of investigation, the official informed me that my sister Freda was living in Dresden. So I went to East Germany as Pieter Van Meer, American. The old Kroner estate was on the road to Dresden, so I stopped there first to visit my wife's grave. My father's mansion was now a rooming house for farm workers and in terrible condition. As I expected, in the Kroner family plot, I found your mother's gravestone overgrown with brush and weeds. After cleaning up the burial site, I went to Dresden. The city's massive scars from the Allied bombing of February 1945 were disappearing." Kroner gulped more water.

"Freda was living in one of those new communist apartments built in the ruins of Dresden. It was a wonderful reunion, because she thought I had been a casualty of the war. We talked about you, and I told her that you had probably been killed in the war. Then someone entered the apartment and I got the shock of my life. It was Sarah.

"This is how Freda and Sarah explained what happened on Christmas Eve 1944. After Ulricht took me to the hospital, my friend Helga found your mother still breathing. One of her friends went and got Freda and a doctor. Helga stayed with her until Freda and the doctor arrived. Since Sarah was Jewish, it would have been impossible to bring her to a hospital. She was taken to the house of one of Freda's friends not far from the estate. That's where the doctor treated her, and that's where she recovered.

"At this same time, I was moved from hospital to hospital as the Russians advanced. The Russians overran the Kroner estate while I was in the hospital. Freda and I never got to communicate directly. However, Martin got back there and saw the freshly dug burial site. Your mother's burial plot was an artifice, a ruse to protect her from the Gestapo. The dirt was only turned up and mounded on the surface; there was no body under it. Later, Freda put up a gravestone to complete the ploy.

"Then the Red Army cut me off from contacting the estate. All communication links were severed. Freda was never able to confidentially communicate to me that your mother was alive. You see, it had to be totally confidential. Just between Freda and me. Directly. Not through Martin, because Freda had hid, protected, and saved a Jew and she was afraid of what the Gestapo would have done if he had found out.

"Then the war ended and the news came out that there were going to be war crimes trials, and Ulricht and I were on the wanted lists. Your mother witnessed Ulricht kill your grandfather. If Ulricht believed she was alive, he would have killed her. It would not have mattered to Martin, even though the war was over. He would have done it."

"Maybe it was Ulricht who shot her?"

"Absolutely not. Ulricht was in the house when the shots rang out. Besides, he had no reason to kill her."

"He sure did. She was a Jew."

"He didn't do it," Kroner said.

"So, you say she is alive and you spoke to her—she must have told you who shot her?"

"She told me that she never saw her assailant, and that she had been awakened by the stallion Hector trampling and snorting. She said she crawled out of the *Manny A.* and climbed down to see why Hector was agitated. Then, she said, she heard a sound in her head, like a shot, or an explosion, and felt herself falling and then blacking out. So, she never saw who shot her."

Ben was sweating, even though the windows and door were open; it was humid inside the cabin. Kroner looked cool, shielding his breast with one bony arm, while occasionally rolling the empty glass of water across his pallid forehead.

Kroner continued, "During the reunion with your mother, a part of me wanted to stay with her, but I had a small child and an American wife I also cared for. No, it would not have been possible to get back together with her, even though I cared for her a great deal. Actually, Manfred, I still loved her. I met her that one time in 1975 and stayed in touch with her, sent her packages and money through an American friend. Because I was a listed war criminal, I did not give her an accurate return address or my most current alias. Naturally, I couldn't tell my new wife about your mother. The situation was quite difficult. I cared for your mother a great deal, but I could not give up my new life and go back to her."

"Why didn't you get her out of East Germany?"

"She did not want to leave, and neither did my sister. In fact, they are living there together now. She will be overwhelmed with joy that you are alive and well. You were almost the entire focus of our conversations because no one knew what had happened to you. We all feared that you had been killed during the final days of the war or ended up as a prisoner of the Soviets.

"I'll give you her address and telephone number in Dresden. It's right in my desk here. We can call her from here. Right now."

"When was the last time you spoke to her?"

"A few weeks ago," Kroner said as he slid open a desk drawer.

Ben tried to recall the details of the last time he saw his mother alive. His memory was in chaos. He couldn't recall her last words to him, and worst of all, he couldn't remember what she looked like or sounded like. His only physical memento of her was a cameo broach of Aphrodite, which he still had.

Kroner came over. "Here is her address and telephone number. She lives in Dresden, near her father's old house. Please call her. Your voice will be a miracle for her."

Ben picked up the telephone and dialed the long series of numbers. He would ask her whose face was engraved on the broach. What kind of broach was it? What was the unique body mark on his cousin Menachem's back? A quarter moon mole. Who was his favorite fictional character? Huckleberry Finn. After a short wait came a long, high-pitched beep.

Kroner took the phone from Ben and listened. "You must have dialed it wrong. Let me try. Read the numbers to me."

Ben watched Kroner dial the numbers carefully as he read them off.

After a while, Kroner said, "Beeping again. I think that beep means the damn East German telephone system has broken down. Here is her address and telephone number; you can try later from your home."

"If you're so afraid of Nazi hunters finding you, why aren't you afraid of being traced back to this phone number?"

"Because I am confident of my identity as Pieter Van Meer." Kroner looked at him in disbelief. "When you talk to her, you will know she is your mother. I want you to understand that I never would have harmed her or you. There are things you don't know about me, about her, about the reason why our family was shattered. You were too young to know. Things you should know, about what happened in the beginning. Please, give me just a few moments to explain."

Chapter 25

Ben turned his back to Kroner, walked over to the window again, and stared out at the lake. The wind was whipping across the water, raising white, foamy welts. In the west, saturated cumulus clouds were broiling upward into the electrified atmosphere.

Ben said, "Go ahead. Talk."

"Thank you, Manfred. I will start by telling you about my father, your paternal grandfather, Baron Manfred Kroner. He was an autocrat, a fanatical Prussian general in the Kaiser's army. I was their only son. All their expectations were directed at me, not at my sister Freda. In 1928, I was sent to the university in Dresden. That is where I met Sarah. She came to play music at our school. She was dark-haired, brown-eyed, and sensual, so different from the German girls with their confident blue eyes, luminous hair, and gleaming teeth. She played the violin better than anyone I had ever heard. I introduced myself to her at the post-recital reception. Immediately, I fell in love with her. Immediately.

"Of course, I couldn't tell my father because he didn't approve of Jews even before Hitler. He wanted me to marry a German, a Lutheran. In Europe, anti-Semitism was well established before Hitler. It just wasn't as brazen and unashamed. It was pan-European, not an exclusively German sickness. However, it was Hitler who made it a state policy to eradicate the Jews. If a Hitler had popped up in Poland, the results could have been very similar. Poles were as anti-Semitic as the Germans, as the Russians, as many other countries.

"But that's well-known history. Anyway, your mother told me that her family wouldn't accept me into her Jewish family, either. In those days, Jews never married Christians. We were in love and blind to the restrictions and traditions around us. We eloped. A judge married us. There was no other way. But it was so very exciting to do it, to be together, in love, young, full of dreams and hopes and ideals, to rebel against traditions. For a while, our parents knew nothing about our elopement.

"I went to work for an engineering company in Hannover. Sarah joined a Hannover orchestra. She wanted to try it a few years. She could always go back to teaching mathematics. We lived in a small apartment. It was a beautiful place. There was classical music always on the phonograph. Good books and an artistic circle of friends, mostly your mother's, small dinner parties and heated arguments about books and artists and music and especially about our abhorrence of the rising interest in the Nazis and Hitler. That was our life.

"Those were the happiest and most passionate days of my life. That's when you were born. 1928. However, when Sarah's father discovered his daughter had married a gentile, he banned her from his house. You were born to parents whose love for each other was true and total. Then, my father also uncovered our secret marriage. He went to your mother's parents. Both fathers agreed that the marriage had to be dissolved, but your mother and I were inseparable. The three of us were inseparable. Our parents' efforts to split us up failed. Our families ostracized us. Then came Hitler's anti-Semitism.

"I lost my job because I was married to a Jew. I lost most of my friends. Your mother lost her friends at the symphony and was asked to leave.

"Shortly after, my father said that I could save myself from economic and social doom if I joined the National Socialist Party and the only way to accomplish this was to leave my wife and child, deny that the marriage ever took place, erase the marriage from all records. Your mother and I did not want to be separated for one minute. All around us Germany was thriving, but we could barely get enough to eat. You were only five years old. We had to do it so I could make money and secretly support the two of you.

"Sarah and I agreed to play along with the separation. We made a pact to meet secretly, communicate regularly. For your sake, your mother and I divorced. My father, with his influence, destroyed the records of our civil marriage. At that time, the SS was recruiting. Candidates had to have a flawless Aryan genealogy. The SS Ancestral Research Unit searched back for Aryan ancestry 175 years. My father had the correct ancestry. I had no problem in getting a perfect genealogy certificate to get into the SS. Our civil marriage ceremony was expunged from all records. A midwife delivered you, so there were no hospital records or a birth certificate.

"Our circle of friends in Hannover had been arrested because of their anti-Nazi, pro-communist stances. Most of them were Jews. They did not turn Sarah in. Officially and legally, our marriage had never taken place. You did not exist. You had no birth certificate. Your mother and I knew that eventually we would be reunited. She took you, and I joined the SS. That was harder than being separated. I had hated Hitler right from the beginning. Now, I had to be among his fanatic SS crowd, cheer with them, laugh and drink with them.

"Sarah's father was a forgiving man. He took her and you back into his home. She lived in his Dresden home with you. Your grandfather Aaron loved you and taught you the things I was not able to. I was very pleased that you were safe in the home of Aaron Henkel."

Ben turned away from the window and sat down in the rocking chair.

"When Hitler assumed power," Kroner continued, "it was against the law for a German to marry a Jew. I never told anyone that I had been married or had a child. I denied your mother and you to safeguard you both. I also knew that to protect you, I would have to become powerful in the SS. In this new life, I could not take a chance and see you. It had to be that way. I wanted desperately to be with you, but I couldn't. I loved you and your mother; I couldn't stop that.

"Our secret meetings stopped. I couldn't write or call. I couldn't take that chance. The SS kept a close watch on their own kind. Exposing me would have meant a promotion for the discoverer. Exposure would have been death for all of us. The struggle to get rank in the SS was very competitive. If the SS had known I had married a Jew, I would have been shot.

"The overwhelming discipline and fanaticism of the SS and the Third Reich supported the denial of my family. Power was there for the taking. I wanted it so I could dictate the terms of my life, because I had none when Sarah and I were forced to part. I wanted it so I could be reunited with you and your mother. Then, a terrible transformation took place. I became infatuated with the power I had as an SS officer. I was lost in its madness. I drowned in its madness. I was above the law and I was corrupted. I became arrogant and cold and powerful. That is what I substituted for losing my family. Even with my new power as an SS Colonel, working directly under

Himmler—especially because I was working so close with Himmler—I couldn't be reunited with you and Sarah.

"So, the Third Reich became my shield, my drug to kill the pain of separation. The power I had sought to bring us back together pulled us apart farther. The Fuehrer was my god. I drank in the hatred. I hated being separated from my wife and my son. I hated myself. I practiced hatred to survive, to live without you. Power and hatred were my beacons.

"Then I went to the school you attended in Dresden, just to see what you looked like. You were ten at the time. It was 1938. When I saw that you had Germanic features, I knew it would be safe to bring you out in the open. I could explain you as a son born out of wedlock to a German woman who was now dead. I wanted to be with you and raise you. It was around this time that I gave you the *MANNY A.* and taught you how to sail it. Secretly, I communicated with Sarah, and we agreed that you would be safer with me. The arrests of the Jews were nearing their peak.

"I assumed responsibility for your upbringing and education. I had to place you in the Hitler Youth camps and was proud of you. Your mother and I agreed to everything. By then, it was getting extremely dangerous for the Henkels to stay in Germany. I shared my predicament with Martin Ulricht. I knew about an American heiress in Marseilles who helped Jews escape to Spain and Portugal and then to the Americas. Your mother did not want to leave Germany because of you. However, I convinced her and all the other Henkels to at least go across the border into neutral Switzerland."

"I think he took them to one of the death camps," Ben said.

" Perhaps he took them to a relocation camp in Germany. Unfortunately, conditions in the camps were deplorable. People died of typhus and malnutrition."

"Deplorable? Six million Jews did not die because of 'deplorable' health conditions. The Nazi death machine, the gas chambers, ovens, and mass executions killed perfectly healthy men, women, and children. You were in the SS. You knew what was going on. Don't insult me and call them relocation camps. Don't lie that you didn't know about the death camps. Ulricht knew about them. He told me there were many. How about Dachau, Bergen-Belsen, Sobibor, Auschwitz? You know all about them. You have been to every one of them."

Kroner placed his palm on his forehead and said, "I'm thirsty." He went into the kitchen.

When he returned, Ben said, "You were always afraid of Martin Ulricht, even though you outranked him militarily. You were too afraid to doubt him or question him."

"He had always carried out my orders precisely. Our relationship was purely military. There was no great friendship."

"I remember that you were very close to Ulricht. You were always together. What happened to that cold-blooded bastard? I hope he took a long time to die."

"He was killed on the Russian front. And yes, you are correct. Martin was a cold-blooded bastard."

"Was his death fake, the same as yours?"

"No. Ulricht is dead, but I got away. The damn communists had me falsely labeled as a war criminal."

"Falsely? So did the West Germans and the Israelis and the Americans and the British."

"Obviously you know something about me. What are they accusing me of?"

"That you murdered Jews. There is paper proof that the Nazis awarded you for your 'psychological discomfort,' the SS medal for the hardships you endured in committing mass murder for the Reich."

"I never received any such award."

"A Nazi hunter has proof you did."

"Who?"

"Hannah Zar. She knew all about you. She confirmed you belonged to the Ring Detachment, a special unit of the SS directly under Himmler. She knew men and women who had witnessed you commit atrocities."

"Lies. I know Hannah Zar. She was your mother's friend. She came to our apartment in Hannover when you were a small boy. She was a fervent Marxist in the '20s. She was a Soviet agent during the war. She became an East German communist who spread lies about Germans who helped American Intelligence to track down and identify communist agents. She said all those Germans were in the SS."

"Hannah Zar had a photograph of you receiving that award. It was part of the evidence at the Nuremberg War Crimes Tribunal."

"That ex post facto proceeding."

"In a civilized society, murder has never been ex post facto."

"Victor's vengeance, then."

"Genocide trumps everything."

"I broke no German law."

"German laws during the Third Reich were inhuman. Under Hitler, it was legal to murder Jews. So, yes, you did not break the insane Nazi law that allowed the murder of Jews, but you broke the laws of a civilized human being. You broke a Commandment of God."

"You twist everything. Lies, lies." Kroner grasped his head. "Manfred, you are my son. I have just told you that your mother is alive. We could be a family again. Let's look ahead and forget the past. I made a huge, tragic, irreversible, misunderstood sacrifice. When you talk to your mother, she will confirm everything I have told you. In the meantime, don't you remember anything good about me?"

"Yes, for years I thought that perhaps you might be dead. Let's not waste time. I don't want to be reunited with you even if she is alive."

"You don't believe me, then?"

"About what?"

"About your mother."

Ben looked away. "I don't remember her voice. That woman in Dresden could be someone pretending she is my mother, some Nazi friend of yours."

"Oh Manfred, no, no. She is your real mother."

"We'll see."

Kroner picked up the phone and dialed the numbers again. After a while he set the phone down. "Something is still wrong on the line. Wait, I want to show you something." He went to his desk and drew out an envelope. "Here is my last month's telephone bill. Look for yourself—you will see I got through to that number." He gave the bill to Ben and took a sip of water, glanced over the rim of the glass, over the clinking ice.

"Why did you assume a new identity if you were not a war criminal?"

Kroner walked closer to Ben. He set the glass of water on an end table. His hands were tightly clasped in the prayer position. He looked like a swimmer in a diving competition, standing on the edge of a diving board. "We must have an understanding. I know that with your hatred for me and your false memories, you could turn me in to the Jewish organizations that hunt Nazis. Because I belonged to the Schutzstaffel, the SS, I fear that I could be accused and deported. To expose former Nazis, the American

Justice Department is going to set up an Office of Special Investigations. Several Nazis have been stripped of U.S. citizenship and deported. Many more are being investigated. The Americans will say I made false statements when I entered the country. I will be stripped of my American citizenship.

"My life will be uprooted, changed forever. I will lose my second family because they know nothing about my past. I know that the Americans will throw me to the dogs, even though it was the American intelligence that gave me a new identity for the purpose of fighting communism. During the war, I spent a great deal of time on the eastern front, interrogating Soviet prisoners. The Americans needed the intelligence I had gathered about the Soviets. But now, most of those Americans are either dead or out of power. All my contacts are gone. Time has abandoned me. Yes, I served in a Death Head unit of the SS, but I did not kill or order one single human being to be killed."

"Liar. You killed my mother. I saw you do it."

"That is not true. I did not kill her. You will see when you speak to her. The Nazi hunters concern me. Being in the SS is enough for them. To them, anyone who served in the SS is guilty of war crimes. The East Germans have extensive files. The Nazi hunters have access to those files."

"Shouldn't they?"

"Some of those files are fake."

"Fake? Why? For what purpose?"

"People are framed all over the world. What difference does it make now? The whole world thinks all the SS were bad."

"They were. Just because some SS daddies played Santa Claus after a hard day of killing Jewish kids, did nothing to change that they were evil," Ben snapped.

Kroner shook his head. "Not everyone pulled the trigger."

"You mean Hitler or Eichmann? Maybe they didn't," Ben said. "But knowingly transporting someone to their death is also murder."

Kroner looked away. "The Nazi hunters will hound me until my dying days. There is no statute of limitations on crimes against humanity, of which I am falsely accused. Only you can prevent this. I have a daughter and a grandchild. They know nothing about my SS past. No one cares or believes that I joined the SS to protect my family. In looking back, I should not have done it. I should have taken you and Sarah out of the country. Every single day of my life, I regret being Hans Kroner the SS officer. He was a despicable human being, but not a war criminal.

"Through my new life, I have paid for the life I led as Kroner. Not a night goes by when I don't think about the things Kroner witnessed and did nothing to stop. Yes, I saw innocent people killed. I saw Russians burned alive and children murdered. Being a witness has left their blood on my hands. I saw crimes and did not lift a finger of protest or try to save a single life. I am guilty of turning my eyes away. After the war, I should have and could have turned in the criminals. I knew so many.

"I want you to know, Ben, that I have broken every link with that past. And I regret that I didn't take you and your mother away from it all. To this day, I wish that I could go back and start my life over again from the day I lost my job because Sarah was Jewish.

"You have to believe me that I have paid for my service in the SS. I am truly sorry for the life I led as Hans Kroner. That is another reason I do not have his name. I desperately want you to believe me. Everything I've said is the truth. I want you to know that the Hans Kroner you knew is dead. I want a chance at becoming friends with you again. I want you back as the son of Pieter Van Meer, not Hans Kroner. I need this chance to show you that I have paid and suffered."

Ben saw his grandmother's and uncles' and aunts' and cousins' faces in the black opening of the SS truck, being taken away to die. Those memories were pervading. The acuteness of his hatred of Kroner was overwhelming, sickening. "It sickens me to think that I'll always be the son of Hans Kroner."

Kroner stepped closer to Ben. His breath was acutely acidic. "I have something to show you. Please wait."

Kroner went to the bookcase. Ben walked toward the door and waited. He glanced around the room. Everything was neat, clean, orderly, smelling of lemon oil, all very tidy and homey. Looking around, he felt no pity for this pathetic man. He was confused as to what he should do about him. First, he would call the number Kroner had given him. Talk to the woman, hear her, listen to her. Then, he would call Hannah Zar. He knew what she would do. Hannah would have her agents check the woman out.

He was staring out over the deep, cool waters of Lake George.

Kroner walked over and gave him a black-and-white photograph. "That is your mother when I first met her in Dresden at the Technological University. It's the only photo I have of her."

Ben had absolutely no memory of what she looked like. He snatched the photograph eagerly. It showed a young woman holding a violin. She had large, dark eyes and curly, black hair. She wore a dark, high-collar dress and a white shawl. To Ben, this woman was a stranger. But then, all at once, he remembered a frightened, sick woman with black circles under her eyes and matted-down straight hair, crying about her father, her body frail and beaten. Ben remembered her face in the motorcycle's sidecar with the wind pushing tears off her cheeks. Pinned to her breast was a cameo broach. It looked very small in the photograph, but Ben recognized it and knew the engraving was of Aphrodite.

He resented Kroner for having known her in that other time, when they were young, before Manfred Aaron was born.

Then Ben remembered sitting with her in the Hitler Youth camp and saw that same broach pinned to her ragged green dress.

"Keep the photo," Kroner said. "It's yours."

Ben stuck the photograph in his pocket. As he walked toward the door, Kroner said, "In the end, you must do what you think is right for you, no matter what the consequences will be."

There was a knock on the screen door. Ben saw a thick-bodied man framed in the screen.

Kroner opened the door to a meaty, smiling face with a gold tooth clamped over a black cigarette holder. "How about a walk, Pieter? We could use the exercise."

"What are you doing here? You were not supposed to return until Monday." Kroner pushed the man back out.

"I came back early because I thought there might be problems."

"There are no problems. I'll see you later, Toby."

"Yes, I suppose for you, later would be better. But for me, there is no better time than the present. Actually, all I wanted to do was help you with your new situation."

"There is no situation, no problem," Kroner said.

Ben could hear that Toby spoke English with an accent very similar to Kroner's—English as spoken by a German. The two men moved farther out on the porch, and one of them spoke in a lowered voice, in a spitting whisper.

Kroner returned with Toby pushing him back into the room. Kroner looked stricken, while Toby smiled willfully, chewed a large wad of pink gum, blew a bubble, and marched into the room.

Chapter 26

Toby said, "Quite extraordinary, Little Max has certainly grown up. And, may I add, very nicely. Ja, ja, very, very."

Kroner spun around and tried to block Toby's further entry into the room, but Toby pushed him out of the way as he blew a flabby, pink gum bubble. After sloppy mouthing the bubble, Toby said to Kroner, "Our bubble is about to burst, Hans. You foolish man, Hans." Then Toby lifted the camera strap over his head and hung a Leica with a telephoto lens on a coat hook on the back of the door. He shut the door and sidestepped around Kroner, who had returned to block him.

Quickly, Toby closed a window and said, "Ay, ay, ay and boy oh boy, did I get an earful. I couldn't help but overhear your very enthusiastic conversation through the open windows. I have been rocking in the rocking chair out on the porch, listening to your cozy family reunion. To say the least, a situation has developed. Houston, we have a problem. Do I get an affirmative on that? Come in, Houston."

"Stop it, Toby." Kroner smiled awkwardly. "There is no problem and please stop this Houston business."

Toby's fleshy face glazed over icily as he closed a second window, turned to Kroner, and said, "As they say here in America, why don't you fornicate with a rolling doughnut, Hans. This is a grave, grave situation. It's shameful and a pity that I was not involved right from the beginning. And this business about your old Jewish wife being alive and you going back to the Fatherland to see her comes as a fatal blow to our lifelong—as you used to say in the old days—esprit de corps. So, we do have a problem, Houston. And that, my friends, is an undeniable affirmative."

Kroner rushed up to Toby, placed his arm around his shoulder and tried to usher him toward the door. "Please excuse us. This is a private matter between me and Mr. Steinhardt."

"Steinhardt, is it?" Toby smirked, but did not budge. He blew a bubble very close to Kroner's face, pushed Kroner's arm away, inserted a cigarette into a black holder and removed a gold lighter from his trousers pocket.

"How does he know your real name is Hans?" Ben asked. There was something familiar about Toby's face. Carve off the fat and age from that corpulent head and who was he? "He addressed you as Hans," Ben repeated. "Don't pretend you didn't hear it."

Toby pushed Kroner away, smiled, and raised his right hand to speak. "Oops, Houston, slipped on that one. A glitch in the switch. So I have, so I did. But zo what. Truth is a sneaky snake now, isn't it? Zo, to clear up the confusion, I will take the floor first."

Kroner extended his arm toward Toby, almost hitting him, holding his palm up as if he were trying to stop something about to strike him. "Halt. Don't you dare."

Toby pushed Kroner's arm to the side. "Be still, Hans," Toby commanded. Then he feigned a few punches, pulled his shoulders back, clicked his heels, flicked open the lighter. After igniting the tip of the cigarette, he removed a pearl-handled Walther pistol from his wrinkled, blue-striped, seersucker sports coat and held it loosely as he swung his heavy arms across his chest. "It's nice to see you again, Manfred, but I fear it's too late to make you shampion of the world. That's a negative on that one, Houston. A negative."

Riled and exasperated, Kroner turned his back to both of them and glared through the picture window.

For Ben, time and corpulence had momentarily camouflaged what Toby's accented utterance "shampion" could not.

Ben knew exactly who Toby was.

Chapter 27

In the predawn of Christmas Day 1944, Manny ran out of the stable and into the woods, where he had parked Stork's motorcycle. To his rear, he heard Ulricht shouting orders. He mounted the BMW's cold, black leather seat, primed and choked the motor, and slammed his foot down on the kick-starter pedal. The cold crankcase oil resisted. As he kicked down again, he looked back and saw two men with flashlights running along the edge of the trees. He kicked the BMW several times before it turned over and caught. As he jammed into first gear and let out the clutch, Rumpel vaulted into the sidecar. As soon as he was out on the old riding trail, he throttled and sped out toward the highway.

As he drove, he could not erase the image of his father standing over his mother with a gun in his hand and the sound of him mumbling, "She is dead, your mother is dead."

His usually keen sense of direction was in disorder. The failure to safeguard his mother was overpowering and relentless. He drove fast and hard, without a bearing or an objective.

In a confused, chaotic state, he kept altering directions, taking turns, breaking and stopping often. In his mind, he returned to the murder scene in the stable, trying to reconstruct it, trying to put it together, to see it all again, to see and remember every detail. But something always seemed to be missing.

It started to snow. Snowflakes stung his face. In each icy sting, he felt her fragile nearness. He heard her call him through the snow that was beating his face and hands. He let it beat him as punishment for not protecting her.

The snow intensified. He was blind and had no direction. Now he was lost. He had taken numerous turns and did not remember any. His mother was just beyond the obfuscating snow, screaming for him to come back and stop her killer.

Overwhelmed, confused, he stopped the motorcycle. He had to go back. She had to be buried according to Jewish customs.

He took an uncertain direction and made risky turns. Speeding around a bend in the road, he lost control of the motorcycle. In the slide and tumble and flip, he and Rumpel were thrown out of the BMW. He skidded through the snow. The sharp, icy gravel cut through his clothes, ripped his skin and dropped him unconscious on the side of the road.

Unscathed, Rumpel licked Manny's scrapes and bruises. The motorcycle lay hissing in the snow.

After a while, he got up slowly, painfully. He was cold; there were bloody snow patches on his clothes. Dizzy and unsure, he stumbled, and walked through the storm with Rumpel by his side. Soon, he saw a light. A house light. He hoped it was Baron Kroner's manor.

He went to the stable and saw that his mother's body had been removed. Only her blanket remained. A discarded death bundle. His body shook from the cold and the huge scrapes on his legs and arms. He wrapped himself in the blanket, lay down on the plank floor, and fell asleep with Rumpel standing watch.

He awoke to the sound of Rumpel barking. He opened his eyes to a bright light and saw a pair of black boots.

"Up, up, Manfred. On your feet," Martin Ulricht said. "Your father has ordered you to go on an important mission for the Fatherland."

A smiling Dieter and Erwin stood behind him. "I pity the Russians Little Max meets up with, don't you?" Erwin said as he and Dieter pulled Manny to his feet.

"Ja, ja," Dieter said. "But it looks like he has already seen battle. Look at that raspberry patch on his leg."

Rumpel's hair was up and he snarled at the SS men. Ulricht pulled out his Luger and fired a round into the floor right in front of the dog. Rumpel leapt at Ulricht. Ulricht sidestepped and fell down, fired again.

Manny shouted, "Run, boy! Run!"

Rumpel darted out of the stable.

Ulricht put his mouth against Manny's ear. "You can have the whole Russian Army now. Your father said you wanted to fight the Russians. Now you will get your chance. Do you know where your father is sending you?"

Manny, still bleary and unfixed on his feet, shook his head.

"Aah, that's goot. It will be a surprise then. You like surprises, don't you Manfred? I'm sure you do. All boys like surprises. It's Yule time and you are going to be a soldier. A little tin soldier. What could be better?"

"What happened to my mother's body?" Manny, suddenly fully awake, acutely angered, demanded.

Ulricht glanced at the other two SS men. "Should we tell him?"

"Let him do his own investigation," Erwin laughed.

Dieter added, "No, no, tell him. Manfred has to know."

"Never mind about his mommy," Ulricht said. "Did you know that Werewolf has a ninety-nine percent casualty rate?"

"What did you do with my mother's body?

"Your Aunt Freda called the Gestapo and they took her away for disposal."

Manny spit in Ulricht's face. He saw Ulricht's huge fist coming toward his face, but couldn't get out of its way.

Chapter 28

The entire Hitler Jugend camp was about to depart for Werewolf, a desperate military operation using teenage boys and girls to fight the advancing Russian army.

Camp Commandant Stork and SS Major Ulricht stood in front of the lined-up boys. Between Ulricht's clenched teeth was an empty, black cigarette holder. Ulricht whispered in Stork's ear. Stork nodded and shouted, "Franz Herbst, front and center!"

A pale and frail fourteen-year-old next to Manny Kroner stepped out of the assemblage and stood at attention in front of Stork and Ulricht.

Ulricht placed one hand on Franz's head and addressed the rest of the boys. "This is your opportunity to defend the Fatherland." Then Ulricht grabbed Franz by the shoulders and swung him around to face the group. "Schoolmaster Stork has informed me that this youth is a coward. Is that true?"

All but Manny shouted, "Jawohl, it's true. He runs from fights. He cries all the time. He's a mama's boy."

Ulricht stabbed a cigarette into the holder, placed it gingerly in the corner of his mouth and lit it. He blew smoke over the back of Franz Herbst's head. Franz could not see the Luger Ulricht removed from his holster. Manny had seen that same pistol commit cold-blooded murder. He could see that Franz had wet his pants, and snot was running out of his nose.

Manny raised his voice above the din. "Sturmbannführer Ulricht, I want to say something."

Ulricht blew more smoke on Franz and shouted, "Speak, Manfred."

Manny suspected what Ulricht was going to do. He had not been able to save his grandfather or his mother, but maybe he could save Franz. He said, "Franz Herbst has a weak body, but his heart is brave. Tell Stork to pair me up with him in Werewolf; I will personally guarantee that he will not be a coward."

"The guarantee of your kind is sheise," Ulricht said. He held the Luger to the back of the shaking boy's head. Franz strained to turn his head, to see what Ulricht had pressed against it. "Manfred Aaron Kroner has guaranteed this youth's courage. Do the young soldiers of the Fatherland agree?"

The boys yelled, "Nein, nein."

Manny yelled, "These mamas boys don't know what courage is. I challenge any one of them to a fistfight with me. Right here and right now."

Ulricht smiled and looked down at Franz. "Manfred is quite the little boxer, as I'm sure you know. Potential shampion, I predict."

Everyone waited. There were no takers.

A boy shouted, "Manfred Kroner sticks up for Herbst all the time."

Another voice, "He fights his fights."

Manny had defended Franz several times and boxed a couple bullies into bloody submission.

Ulricht looked down at Franz. "Germans have to fight their own battles." Then he addressed the assemblage. "This youth is the only coward in this unit." He cocked the pistol and shot Franz in the back of the head. "Now there are no cowards in this unit."

Then he stepped over the twitching, bleeding body of Franz Herbst and came up to Manny. "Fight, Manfred. Fight and after the war, I'll make you shampion of the world." Then Ulricht whispered in his ear, "Between you and me, Manfred, if you can survive Werewolf's ninety-nine percent casualty rate, you will truly be a shampion."

Chapter 29

The approaching thunderstorm dimmed the light over Lake George.

"Shampion of the world?" the corpulent man repeated. "Don't you remember me?" Toby asked. "I am Martin Ulricht. I used to call you Little Max Schmeling. I have had you in my thoughts for forty years, ever since I left you in the Fuehrer's youth camp. Pleasure to meet you again." Ulricht clicked his heels and thrust out his hand.

Ben glared at Kroner. "Broken all your Nazi ties? Ulricht doesn't look very dead to me."

"This is a private matter, Toby," Kroner said, avoiding Ben's punitive look.

"There are no private matters between us, Hans," Ulricht interrupted, waving the pistol at Ben. "Don't try one of your escapist tricks on me, Manfred. I deal swiftly with disorder. This predicament, Hans, really concerns me."

"You don't need that pistol to keep me here. I have no intention of leaving," Ben said.

"Please, Toby," Kroner said.

"Shtop this Toby business, this Mr. Van Meer and Mr. Steinhardt kaka. I'm Martin and your Hans and he's Manfred. We're reunited again. We can revel in old memories. There's no need to pretend in front of Manfred. It's time we are all our true selves. I overheard your emotional discussion, and it's clear to me that your differences are too extreme to be synchronized— or is it synthesized. Which is correct, Little Max? Feel free to shtop and correct my American. Perhaps I should say eye to eye.

"Zo, Hans, Little Max, what should we do? This is a very grave situation. Don't you agree, Hans? Don't you also agree, Manfred, that the sheise has hit the fan. I would have no problems with this unexpected evolvement if it weren't for the fact that Hans is my lifelong friend and you are his son."

Kroner folded back onto the couch and dropped his head in his hands, mumbling, "This is my son. You never had children, so you wouldn't understand. You should not have come in here. You should not have revealed yourself to Manfred. Everything was going to work out." Kroner stared at the floor. "And please put that damn gun away. There won't be any need for any guns."

But Ulricht's gun arm shot out and his grimace stiffened. He pointed the gun at Ben. "Bist du positiv, Hans? Sit down, Little Max. We all have to talk, heart to heart, a good old-fashioned bull session. You will see, Hans, that your best interests will be served. Do you think that once you two are reconciled that your life as Pieter Van Meer and mine as Toby Johanson will be okay and just so very fine again?

"Keep in mind that we have always been a team. Our lives are one life, not two. We are fugitive Siamese twins, Hans, shackled together with the bloodhounds of our past still on our trail. And one of those hounds has just arrived. From what I have heard through the open window, I conclude that our play was heading for a command performance before a Jewish judge in Tel Aviv. I had to step in because you were arranging our one-way trip to the Jewish gallows. You were going to wreck everything we have spent a lifetime building. Hans, you are slipping in your golden years. You are running on empty, as they say here in America. Our bond should always be the closest to your heart, not some impure and illegal biological link. We are the two inseparables, Hans, not you and Manfred."

"Er ist mein Sohn, Martin. My son."

Ulricht smirked. "Of course he is your son, Hans. You didn't choose each other, but we did. Can't you comprehend that something of a much more serious nature has developed precisely because of that biological link? Of course you can be reunited. Here in this cabin only, and for now only. Never beyond, and never again. But there is another matter that also concerns me. This covert business about your trip back to the Fatherland and this nonsense about your first wife being alive upsets and angers me. I have never been so angry with you, Hans."

"It is the truth," Kroner said. "She is alive. In 1975, you went to that big Wermacht reunion in Toronto. My daughter couldn't come to visit me that week, so I decided to fly out to see her. Remember? I told you I was flying out to see my daughter. Instead of flying to California, I flew to Germany to see my sister Freda."

"Freda? Are you crazy? You went to see Freda?" Ulricht shook his head as Kroner explained how his wife survived and how he had learned about it. Disgusted, he looked away from Kroner. "I saw her dead, and Manfred saw her dead. Your family doctor pronounced her dead. Her killer was executed. Stop making up stories about her being alive. It's not possible. It was extremely reckless to go back to the Fatherland and see Freda. Do you know how dangerous that was?"

"It wasn't that dangerous," Kroner said. "Do you remember Heinrich Strasser?"

"Yes, of course. How could I forget one of our old SS boys?"

"He became a big shot in East German intelligence. For years, Strasser and I were in secret communication. I wanted him to find my sister Freda. About one month before my return, Strasser notified me that Freda was living in Dresden under a new name, because the Kroner name was too closely connected to the SS. It seems like everyone is living under false appellations. Strasser got me into East Germany. My first visit was to my wife's grave at the old Kroner manor."

"How could you have meetings with Strasser and not tell me? We have always shared everything." Ulricht turned his back to Ben and waved the pistol angrily at the ceiling. "That trip to East Germany could have been the end of both of us. The truth is, Strasser was a weasel. How do you think he got to be a communist agent? You can't trust a red weasel. If you had been caught, I know you would have exposed me.

"Did you forget that I saved your life? Your leg had only been removed from the infection your own son gave you when he struck you with that ax and all that horseshit got in your blood. I carried you out of the back door of the hospital when the Russians were coming in the front. I burdened my own escape to save you, my lifelong comrade. How could you go back and have these communications behind my back? I stayed by your side every moment and kept nothing from you."

"You stayed with me more than thirty years ago, Martin, because you needed me. I had a lot of money and I had contacts. You were a low-class person of no significance. You needed me more than I needed you. You don't know anything about money even today. You can't even figure out a restaurant check or how to make change right here in America. You knew it was going to take a lot of money to get away and evade arrest. I made payments. I shifted accounts in Switzerland, Argentina, Mexico, here in

America. I bought visas and passports and identities and safe places to live. Brute force would not have gotten us very far. You had no understanding in these matters.

"Look, Martin, we haven't been caught for all these years. I know you would have done everything in your power to stop that trip. I had to do it secretly."

Ulricht grabbed Kroner by the collar and spoke inches from his face. "You skulked away, you put us in danger, you could have put a Jewish noose around our necks."

At that moment, Ben sprang at Ulricht, knocked the pistol out of his hand, and smashed his fist into Ulricht's face. He felt the fat man's nose collapse. Ulricht fell to the floor, and Ben lunged on top of him. Ulricht struggled and covered his face with his hands and tried to use his weight to turn over, but Ben sat on his chest and pounded the fat man's face with his fists, which turned bloody from Ulricht's mushy and lacerating skin.

Ulricht heaved his chest and tried to throw Ben off. He flailed his arms and yelled, "Help me, Hans! Get this shit off me!"

Ben looked up and saw Kroner approaching quickly. He didn't have time to react as Kroner jammed a small black cylinder into his chest. Ben felt a shock. *An electrical jolt,* Ben thought as everything went black.

Chapter 30

When Ben regained consciousness, he was lying on the hearth.

"Rise and shine, Little Max. Are we awake? Come, come, now, wake up," Ulricht said while holding a bloody white towel against his nose.

Ulricht, hacking and spitting, his nose a bloody mess, yelled at Kroner, "Sheise. Sheise. Shit, Hans."

Kroner ran off into the kitchen and returned with a clean towel that he gave to Ulricht, whose nose and one eyebrow still bled.

While blotting the blood, Ulricht said, "Give me the little stun gun, Hans."

"He's had enough."

"Give it to me." Ulricht held out his hand.

"For what?"

"A little jolt while we decide things. Come on, Hans. Stop pissing around. Give me the damn thing."

From his trouser pocket, Kroner withdrew a six-inch-long, black plastic cylinder. He moved it up closer to his eyes and turned a small dial. "This is the minimal dose. "

Ulricht grabbed the cylinder out of Kroner's hand. "This is one of your father's inventions. He's so good wiz ze gadgets. Watch." Ulricht jammed it into Ben's chest. Ben slumped back.

Kroner walked over to the hearth and closed the gate in the center. Once he locked the gate, Ben was a prisoner on the fireplace hearth.

"You're in the doghouse now, Little Max." Ulricht picked up a sheathed filet knife from the coffee table. "What was your son going to do with this, Hans?"

Ben's shoes and socks had been removed before he was moved to the hearth, to make him a better conductor of electricity if he touched the spark screen while attempting to jump over.

"This is no simple dog pen. I have an added feature," Kroner said as he placed his hand on the top of the five-foot-high screen and shook it. "This is no simple spark screen. It is high and strong. Come here, Martin, I want to demonstrate something. Put your hand right here where mine was."

Ulricht came over. Kroner walked over to the bookcase, removed a book, and flipped a switch. Martin jumped back, jolted by the electric current.

"My, my, Hansie, another surprise. You little Einstein, you. All that's missing is the guard tower. But goot, goot, we have our little concentration camp right here on your hearth, with an electric fence and a convenient fireplace oven right behind it. Very nice."

Kroner, still standing by the bookcase, said, "You got the twelve-volt DC dose. This next switch jumps the voltage up to 110 AC. When the 110 is on and you touch the screen, it will knock you down."

Ulricht glanced at Ben, who was starting to stir.

Kroner walked over and checked the padlock on the gate.

"That is by far your best invention," Ulricht said. "A spark screen that makes its own sparks."

Kroner grabbed the stunner out of Ulricht's hand.

"Leave the 110 on," Ulricht said.

"Of course." Kroner walked over to the bookcase and did exactly the opposite—he switched off the 110-volt circuit and turned on the twelve-volt.

As Ben sat up, Ulricht led Kroner out of earshot. They spoke in lowered voices. In German.

Kroner stood with his head down, staring at the floor, shaking his head.

Ben hadn't heard German in many years. If they had been within earshot, he would have understood them.

Ulricht walked back in the room and sat down with his head back. His nose had started to bleed again. Kroner went into the kitchen and returned with a glass of water.

Ulricht got up and said, "I'm going to wash my face."

When he was upstairs and the faucet was running, Kroner said to Ben, "Be careful. Don't touch the spark screen. It's 110 volts."

Ben sat up with his back against the cobblestone.

Kroner said, "I need to know about Werewolf. I gave Martin specific instructions. Werewolf was certain death. I never would have sent you to die."

Ulricht came back down the stairs and asked, "What are you chatting about?" There were blood smudges on his jaw and neck.

"Werewolf."

"Manfred survived Werewolf. It would be interesting to find out how he did it. Tell us, Manfred. How did you do it? It must be one hell of a fine adventure."

"I had a damn good reason to live," Ben said.

"What was that?" Kroner asked.

"To find and kill you two bastards."

Chapter 31

Ulricht shouted as he stepped into the car, "I vill make you champion of the world, Little Max."

As the car sped out of the youth camp, Stork ordered the boys to drag Franz Herbst's body away and said to Manny, "So, Kroner, it looks like Commandant Ulricht is not such a good uncle. I'm going to make you pay for the BMW motorcycle you stole and ruined. You are under my command now, and for you I will have a special assignment right away."

An hour later, Manny was in a truck heading toward the advancing Red Army. Two ten-year-old boys were singing a song about being brave soldiers for the Fatherland. Manny couldn't forget Franz's face just as Ulricht pulled the trigger. Swollen tears rolled down his cheeks, his body trembled inside the oversized uniform and lace-less shoes. Snot crept out of his nose. He gave a brave smile for the boys watching, the boys who hated him and left him out of their games, who ridiculed him ceaselessly. Manny recalled when Franz's widowed mother had visited her only child and how terrified she had been of the other boys and the teachers.

Several hours later, the truck stopped in a small town. Artillery thudded and flashed nearby. The boys were herded into a barn, where Hitler Jungmaedel were handing out clothing taken from dead Russians.

A sad, blue-eyed BDM girl held up an oversize Russian peasant shirt for Manny. "How old are you?"

"Sixteen," Manny said.

"You look older."

He smiled. "You like seventeen better? Or maybe eighteen? Maybe twenty-one? What do you like?" Since the experience with Helga, Manny had a newfound confidence.

She smiled, but there were tears welling in her eyes. "I'm seventeen, and there isn't much chance that I'll ever see eighteen or see my mutti again. The Russians will overrun us by morning. That's what I heard. We're just here to divert the Russians so the adult SS units have time to plug up more important holes in the defense."

"Or give them time to run away."

"I've seen what the Mongols do to even younger girls than myself."

"What's your name?" Manny asked.

"Erika. And yours?"

"Manfred. Everyone calls me Manny."

"Manny," she said tentatively, thoughtfully. Her smile was blue and rueful, a wilted flower in a cracked vase.

When she referred to her mother as "mutti," she sounded like a frightened child. Manny was tugged into her disconsolation. It forced him to think about his own mother, something he had been desperately trying not to do. Erika's shoulders slumped and her hands fidgeted with the shirt. Her eyes were dire and dark, like his mother's had been, like more and more German people. *If Germany had eyes,* he thought, *and it looked into a mirror, the reflection would be desolation, horror, and fear.*

"Have you seen the Russians?" he asked.

She looked down and dropped the shirt on the floor. Manny picked it up. She stared straight ahead past him, toward the door through which streamed German boys dressed as Russian peasants. "I saw Mongols. In a dorf a few days ago, a shell hit the house where we were sleeping and everybody—everybody—was killed or wounded."

Erika held back the tears. "I was under a section of a floor that fell. When I regained consciousness, through the cracks in the floor, I saw the Mongol soldiers raping the wounded and even the dead girls. All of them. My friends Marta from Hannover, Maria from Gottingen, Heidi of Koln— another Heidi was from Danzig. Maria was from Leiptzig. And I forgot Marlena from Dusseldorf—she was more beautiful then Marlena Dietrich."

She started to sob uncontrollably. "They were all raped and then killed with bayonets. And I escaped. I am alive for what purpose? For what end? To be raped and killed? To never see my mutti again? I can't bear to think that my mutti will never see me again. They tell us every day to be faithful and pure and German? Why? Why can't it just end? I am sick of being faithful, pure, and German."

Manny knew that "Be Faithful, Be Pure, Be German" was the Hitler Youth motto for girls, as for the boys it was "Live Faithfully, Fight Bravely, and Die Laughing." He put his arm around Erika and she dropped her head on his shoulder. Manny said, "And above all, stay alive. Be faithful, be pure, and stay alive. That's my version. I don't want to die laughing. I want to live laughing. Only an insane person dies laughing."

Through subdued sobbing, she smiled valiantly. Manny saw Stork coming toward them. Manny said to Erika, "Here comes that dumpkopf

Stork." She pulled back and wiped away her tears with the back of the hand and smiled. Manny asked, "Do you want to run away from all this?"

Between the sobs, she said, "We can't. Why would you? They will shoot us if we try."

"So you don't care if the Russians shoot you, just as long it's not the SS. What's the difference who kills you? On the brighter side, if the SS shoots you, at least you will not be raped. I will be—they like boys better."

"I wouldn't know which way to run. The fighting is all around us."

"Leave that up to me."

Manny saw Commander Stork standing at attention and clicking his heels while being dressed down by a Waffen SS officer.

"How can we get away? There is no way."

"That's why I joined Werewolf," Manny lied. "What do you think? No one forced me into this. I knew that Werewolf would provide opportunities for escape that I didn't have at the youth camp."

"You made a terrible mistake. No one gets away from Werewolf alive."

"We will. Be ready. I'll come to get you."

She looked over him to locate Stork. "When? I have to know. When?"

"Tonight."

"I can't bear this another second. I want to go home."

"Where do you live?"

"In Dresden."

"I'm from Dresden."

"You are?"

"I lived there. I know how to get there. I know Dresden like the back of my hand. Where will you be tonight?"

"Here. We are sleeping in this barn unless the Russians break through and drive us away or kill us."

Manny glanced around. "Sleep there, near the door."

"I won't sleep. I'll wait with my eyes open. Do you know which way to go?"

"Of course. Dresden is that way, west. I lived there for many years. I know this countryside. I had an uncle who lived near this very place."

Stork's voice cut into their plans. "Kroner, Manfred. Froehm, Alfred. Sprung auf, marsch, marsch. By the exit. At once."

Erika dropped her eyes. Manny felt her desperate look go right through him. He said, "I'll come to get you."

She reached out and touched his hand. "Please, come back. I have to get away from here."

"Kroner, Manfred, by the exit at once!" Stork shouted.

"Dresden has not been bombed, and it won't be because it's a city with no military value. I'll be back later tonight." Manny ran off and didn't look back, carrying with him Erika's dispirited comely face, her blue, melancholy eyes. He swore he would see her again before dawn.

Chapter 32

Stork had already picked out ten other boys, including Manny.

The boys were issued German grenades, Russian rifles, and several pistols. Stork asked, "Who can shoot with a pistol?"

Manny raised his hand. Stork gave Manny an old Russian revolver.

"How about a Luger?" Manny asked. "I know how to use one."

"Russian peasants aren't issued German Lugers. A good German soldier will adapt to any situation."

"What about ammunition. This gun is not loaded."

Stork smiled. "Presently, we're all out of Russian ammunition. You'll just have to get it from the Russians."

"How am I supposed to do that? Just tap a Russian on the shoulder and ask him? 'Ah, excuse me, comrade Boris, can I borrow some bullets from you? I'd like to load my pistol so I can shoot you in the ass.'"

No one laughed. All of them were too scared.

"Kill one and take his," Stork said.

"With what?"

"Use your fists. You say you are a boxing champion."

The boys laughed.

Stork reached in his pocket and gave Manny one cartridge.

Manny was paired with a twelve-year old boy. His name was Alfred Froehm, and he had just peed in his pants. Manny moved a few steps away from him. Alfred could barely carry the four grenades, hanging from straps around his neck and the rusty Russian rifle with three rounds of ammunition, one seized in the chamber. He hoped it would dislodge upon firing. Manny took two grenades to lighten Alfred's load.

The boys were taken to different points along the front positions, in a sector defended by the Waffen SS. Manny saw that some of the adult soldiers were not much older than him.

A Waffen SS captain with his arm in a sling and a bandage around his head said to them, "There's a machinegun in the cellar of that house. It is blocking a strategic road we need to open." He pointed across the field in front of them. "We have no mortars or artillery and no tanks. Your job is to knock it out with grenades."

Manny glanced at the house, the length of two football fields away. Suddenly, fear rushed through him. "I can't throw a grenade that far."

The captain smiled. "Of course not from here. You have to get closer and toss it through the back window."

"That's insane."

"No, that's war, and that's what you have to do for the Fuehrer. Do it, or I will not hesitate to shoot you."

Manny envisioned Erika waiting for him; that was all the incentive he needed.

"Give me some more grenades," Manny said. "I'm ready to blow up some Russians."

"That's the spirit."

The captain gave Manny four more grenades and said, "Some of them are duds. You might just as well throw all of them."

The boys were taken to a nearby swamp and instructed to go straight through. On the other side would be a field where they would proceed north about 200 meters. They would wind up about 100 meters behind the house.

"Good luck, boys," the captain said. "Get that machine gunner or don't come back."

Manny walked ahead of Alfred. The swamp was icy and thick with brush. In a small clearing, they found the frozen bodies of several bayoneted and shot Russian and German soldiers. Manny looked for more ammunition among the dead bodies, but their uniforms were frozen solid, and he couldn't open their pockets or look inside their clothes. Their faces were white and frosty, and their bodies lay in a grotesque heap. Manny was thinking about his mother, while next to him Alfred trembled with cold and fear.

When they got to the edge of the swamp, Manny said, "You stay here, Alfred. I'll take care of the machine gunner. You watch my behind."

Manny made sure there was a cartridge in the rifle's magazine. He took all the grenades and ran off along the edge of the swamp. There was a small rise covered with evergreens. He crawled under the trees and came to the top. Beyond, the country opened. He could see the house. Two Russian soldiers were standing outside. To attack the house from the rear, across an open field, was suicidal.

Then he saw movement. Two boys from the school were running toward the house from an oblique direction but still across the edge of the open field. One boy wore a bright red shirt, the other a ripped Russian karakul coat. One of the soldiers spotted them just as the karakul boy threw a grenade. The grenade exploded and killed one soldier and knocked the other one down. When the soldier tried to get up, the red-shirted boy ran up to him and stuck a bayonet in his stomach, then his throat.

The karakul boy attempted to open the door of the house, when suddenly the door shattered from the inside and the boy fell dead. The red-shirted boy ran toward the door and threw a grenade inside. When the grenade did not detonate, he rushed into the house. A few moments later, the red-shirted boy was dragged outside by two Russian soldiers. One soldier held the boy's hands behind his back while the other cut his throat.

Manny didn't wait long to make a decision. He ran back to the swamp and found Alfred, who was sitting in the snow shivering.

They ran deep into the swamp and crawled under low evergreen branches. "We'll rest for an hour," Manny said. "Then, we'll get away."

"Get away? We have to go back to our unit and fight on."

"Fight? Are you crazy? You don't sound like you believe your own words."

"We have no choice. We were ordered by the Fuehrer."

"I'm not fighting for that lunatic, Hitler."

"You shouldn't say that about our Fuehrer. I don't think you should talk about running away. You saw what happened to Franz. We have to go back. We did our job, now we have to do another one."

"Some of the boys were killed already. I saw it. They cut Otto Heider's throat, and Gerhard was killed by a machine gun. They're dead. Do you know what it means when you're dead? You can't eat or play or fart or pee in your pants or make love to women. Do you understand that? I'm through fighting."

"You're a coward. You saw what happened to Franz."

"I don't care. At least I'll be alive. If you want to live, you have to run. Be faithful, be true, and run for your life. That's my motto."

"Are you sure?" Alfred asked.

"Positive. Now rest up."

When Manny awoke, Alfred was gone. Angry with himself for falling asleep, Manny scrambled and crawled out from under the thick brush onto crusty snow and full moonlight. He heard shooting all around him.

Because of the light reflecting off the snow, visibility was good, especially across the open fields. He came to the edge of the swamp and thought he detected movement near the evergreens. It was a dog and it loped like Rumpel. He wanted to call out, but the dog suddenly darted under the thick undergrowth.

Manny ran across the field until he reached the cover of the evergreens again. Under the entangling branches, he called out, "Rumpel, here boy. It's Manny, here boy."

The dog didn't respond.

He waited and listened but heard nothing. He moved ahead through the trees and quickly came to the edge, looking for the dog. He had two grenades. The house he had been ordered to attack looked like it was still held by the Russians. Several bodies lay near the door. Manny saw that there were more than before, and they were small bodies—not the bodies of men, but boys.

Then he saw movement. A dog, an Alsatian who loped and darted like Rumple was running across the field toward the house. He was pretty sure it was Rumpel. Manny wanted to shout out his name, but held back. Rumpel was now in the back of the house, sniffing around the bodies. Manny saw that there were at least seven dead boys littered around the back of the cabin, lifeless, freezing clumps of landscape, like the bodies in the swamp, entwined in the surroundings as if the dead had to camouflage themselves from the living.

In a lowered voice, Manny called out to Rumpel. Rumpel kept sniffing, going from body to body. Then the door opened and one of the Russians came out. He raised his gun and aimed it at Rumpel. In full voice, Manny yelled out, "Rumpel, behind you boy!"

The Russian looked toward the evergreens and swung his rifle around. Rumpel rushed the Russian and knocked him down. The Russian got up and ran inside with Rumpel in pursuit.

Manny heard shots fired inside the house. He ran toward the house and stood by the door with a hand grenade, pin out, ready to throw. He shouted, "Out Rumpel, out! Come out to Manny! Come on, Rump. Come on boy."

Rumpel bolted through the doorway. Manny threw the grenade through the opening. It exploded immediately, and he felt an implosion inside his head as if his eardrums had been crushed. He threw in the other grenade and held his hands over his ears as he waited for the detonation.

When the smoke and dust cleared and he opened his eyes, Manny saw the SS captain who had sent him on the mission standing over him. "Good work, good work. We had a bad report about you. Trooper Alfred said you were a coward and that you tried to get him to run away with you."

"Alfred said that? As you can see, that's not true. I was just waiting for the right opportunity. Alfred had pissed in his pants and maybe had done even more. He smelled pretty bad. I had to get rid of him. I was afraid the Russians would smell our attack."

The Waffen SS men laughed and told him he was a hero of the Fatherland.

The captain pointed at Rumpel. "Where did the Alsatian come from?"

"He's mine," Manny said. "Actually, he's my father's, Standartenfuhrer Kroner."

"You are Hans Kroner's son? Does he know you are with Werewolf? It's suicide," he laughed.

"Back where they issue orders, some pencil pusher made a big mistake," Manny said. "I don't understand what my father's dog is doing here. Rumpel is with my father all the time."

"A hospital is no place for dogs."

"The hospital?"

"Did you know your father was wounded in action?" the captain said. "He's in a nearby field hospital. But don't be too concerned, as I heard that Standartenfuhrer Kroner has only a foot wound."

"I would really like to go see him," Manny said.

"Of course. I'll have someone drive you there. You have done a heroic deed for the Fatherland. And I don't want to be the commander of a unit where Hans Kroner's son was killed. Your father has a great deal of power and influence in high places. Go see your father, and he'll get you out of this hellhole."

The captain wrote a note describing Manny Kroner's heroic act and gave it to him. "If I am killed, this letter will get you a decoration. Also, I am giving you a battlefield commission. You now have the rank of Sergeant, and you will be issued a uniform of the Waffen SS."

At the SS supply truck, while waiting for a ride to the hospital, Manny put on a used uniform. He felt strange and powerful in the slightly oversized SS garments, boots, and insignia. Rumpel barked at him, not recognizing him in the uniform. In front of the building was a motorcycle and sidecar. The lieutenant inside had said Manny would get a ride to the hospital in three or four hours. In three hours, it would be light. Manny pushed the motorcycle away from the building.

Rumpel hurdled into the sidecar as Manny kick-started the BMW. With murder on his mind, he drove east, toward the hospital that was in the opposite direction of the village where Erika was waiting. Manny had passed that village on the way to the supply center. He estimated the distance to it was about five kilometers. The hospital was about ten kilometers away in the opposite direction. With only two or three hours of darkness remaining, he changed his mind and decided to liberate Erika first, and go to the hospital afterwards.

The small bridge he had crossed only an hour before had been blown up, and Wermacht troops told him there was another bridge about nine kilometers west. After crossing that one, he had to find roads going east. He also needed petrol.

He saw two military trucks turning into a dirt road; one of them was either a water or gasoline pumper. Shortly, an SS guard at a barbed wire gate stopped the trucks.

Manny pulled up to the gate. "I need petrol."

The SS guard directed him inside the barbed wire compound. He was instructed to park the motorcycle next to the pumper truck and told that there would be about a fifteen-minute wait until the pump's hose was repaired.

An SS officer holding a megaphone asked him, "I see you are a soldier of the Waffen SS. Tell me, how far away are the Russians?"

"Right in our own backyard." Manny glanced around and asked, "What is this place? A prisoner of war camp?"

"Look for yourself. It will be gone in a few days. Not a trace left."

"A trace of what?"

The officer smiled. "Look and you will understand."

Chapter 33

To the left was a single barracks. To the right was a large brick building with a flat roof and a black metal chimney. In the bright moonlight, Manny saw about a hundred ragged men huddled against the wall of the brick building with several SS guards standing around them. At one end of the building was a stack of sledgehammers, shovels, and picks. One face reminded Manny of his cousin Menachem.

The SS officer raised the megaphone to his mouth. Manny walked closer to the group of men, to look at the faces, at the man who looked like his cousin Menachem. Could it really be him?

The officer said, "Because of air raids, we will be working by the light of the moon only. You will start by taking down the chimney first. Then, you will take the roof and wood rafters down and make a neat stack of the timbers. Brick walls come down next. The mortar will all be removed from the bricks and they will be neatly stacked in cubes of 400 over there. After the building is down, we will remove the barbed wire and the posts. The wire will be neatly rolled, the posts will be stacked with the other timbers, all the nails pulled out, hammered straight, sorted, and boxed by size."

Manny looked at the tomblike, starved faces. He stepped closer to the man who looked like Menachem.

Manny asked, "What's your name?"

"Jacob. Do you know me?"

"I thought I did. I thought you were my cousin Menachem."

"Why would an SS man have a cousin named Menachem? All Menachems are Jews. It is obvious you're not a Jew."

"My mother was a Jew."

"Does your mother know her Jewish son is in the SS?"

"No."

"You should be ashamed."

"It's a temporary uniform."

"You're a bad Jew, and God will hate you for all time."

Manny sensed that Jacob was fearless.

"That gun in your holster gives you power," Jacob said. "Because your mother is a Jew, you are a Jew. Help your people the Jews. Give me your gun. Then, you will not be hated by God." Jacob spit on the ground. "We were marched here from Auschwitz-Birkenau. A hundred died on the way. Do you know about Auschwitz-Birkenau? It's an extermination camp. Have you heard about sonderbehandelt wurden? It's the Special Handling operation, the gassing and cremation of all Jews. Remember that term. Sonderbehandelt wurden has killed almost every Jew in Europe. What was your mother's maiden name?"

"Henkel."

"Remember what I say, Henkel. Remember me, Henkel. I, Jacob Abramowitz, sondercommando dragged the bodies out of the gas chambers and threw them in the ovens. Thousands upon thousands, Henkel. One of them could have been a Henkel. Millions of Jews were exterminated. Now, the SS is destroying the death camp. We are here to tear this place down. They don't want the world to know what they did here, even though by their standards, this was a mediocre facility—only 50,000 exterminated here in this place, just an overflow death camp.

"After we tear down this place, they will kill us. But I don't care, as long as I can kill a few of them bastards. So give me your gun, Henkel, and I'll start with that guard over there. I saw him shoot children in front of their mothers." Jacob held out his hand.

Manny stepped back.

Jacob spat on the ground and said, "This moment has marked you forever in the eyes of God. You have failed to save a fellow man, a fellow Jew, and God was a witness."

"With my one gun, you have no chance to defeat the SS."

"For years I have survived in the death camps because I believed that someday I would get to take revenge. Your refusal makes my years of survival wasted. Because of you, I have lived through hell for nothing. I know I can't defeat the entire SS. All I want is to kill a few of those murdering bastards. I know God has sent me this opportunity. You are God's messenger. Help me. Give me the gun. It's not your gun anyway. It belongs to God."

The megaphone resonated. "The railroad tracks and ties will be the final part of your job. When everything is finished, you will be free to leave. Do a good job. A Schutzstaffeln field kitchen will be here around noon today to provide you with a hearty meal. So, get to work. The sooner you finish doing a thorough job, the sooner you will be free."

The prisoners picked up the tools and climbed a ladder leading to the roof.

Jacob held out his hand.

"They will shoot you."

"Good. I want to die fighting."

Manny backed away.

Jacob pleaded, "Let me have the death that I have lived for."

An SS guard ran over and pushed Jacob away.

A few minutes later, there was shouting. Manny saw Jacob standing on the roof, addressing the other men in Yiddish. "Refuse to work. Refuse to destroy this place of genocide. We have to fight to preserve this place. They will kill us when we are done. No one will remember what happened here. We have to fight to preserve this killing ground of thousands of Jewish men, women, and children. The Soviet army is not far. Let's fight and hold this place until they arrive."

A guard asked Manny, "Do you know what he is saying?"

Manny said, "When I was a boy, I lived next to Jews. I learned some Yiddish." On purpose, Manny translated Jacob incorrectly. "I think he's trying to rouse his men to work hard, to do a good job."

The guard smiled smugly. "Smart Jew."

As Manny walked away, he heard a commotion and saw Jacob climb down the ladder with several other men approaching the stacked shovels and hammers. Manny heard them whispering in Yiddish. The SS guards started shouting at them. Then suddenly, Jacob's small group grabbed shovels and sledgehammers and rushed toward an SS guard. They knocked him down. Jacob grabbed the guard's rifle and shot one of the SS men.

Manny stood frozen as Jacob fell in a hail of bullets. The uprising was over. The other Jews were backed up against the building and held at bay.

Chapter 34

Manny and Rumpel approached the village carefully, stopping and turning off the motorcycle to listen for sounds of aircraft, tanks, voices, and gunfire. The barn where Erika waited was just beyond the church, its spire piercing the moonlit night. The air was pale and still; he felt light and indestructible and knew he would have to be swift and deft.

He concealed the motorcycle behind a hedge and ran into town, dodging and crouching behind buildings and darting through alleyways. Rumpel suddenly stopped and looked up at the hills to the east. Manny heard a distant motor starting up, then a few more. The sound came from somewhere behind the rising hill to the east of the village, beyond which was the Russian army.

A door slammed shut nearby, and he saw several Wermacht soldiers running down the main street. The sound of motors grew louder. Several loud explosions went off very close. The earth shuddered under his feet.

He ran up to the barn, opened the door and peered inside. In the darkness, he saw sleeping bodies covered with blankets. Erika was sitting up. She sprang to her feet. Manny took her hand and they ran out. All around them, shouting soldiers ran toward the south end of town. The motor sound grew louder still.

"What's going on?" Manny asked one of the soldiers.

"Russian tanks have broken through."

Erika ran back to the barn, flung the door open, and shouted inside, "Everybody up! Get up. Get up. Russian tanks, Russian tanks!"

The girls rushed out of the barn. Erika ran around shaking the sleepy stragglers. Manny pulled her away, and they ran west between houses, through yards and gardens, to the hedgerow where he had left the BMW.

The first shell hit between the church and the barn. Then a barrage of shells landed directly on the barn. Erika stopped and looked back. Manny dragged her along the hedgerow, telling her to stay low. When they glanced back, they saw the town being shelled by the tanks that had lined up on the hill. Civilians and soldiers were streaming out of town. Russian infantry were now running down the hillside. The barn, the church, and several other buildings were engulfed in flames.

Manny started the motorcycle. Erika slid into the sidecar. A round from one of the Russian tanks exploded nearby, then another close enough for them to feel the shockwave of the blast. Rumpel jumped into Erika's lap as Manny let out the clutch and turned the throttle. The rear wheel spun and the motorcycle lurched forward as a shell exploded on the spot they just departed. The blast nearly knocked them over.

Out of tank range, Manny braked suddenly and pulled the motorcycle off to the side of the road. Hundreds of refugees were scrambling into the ditch along the road and lying down, seeking cover from a low-flying fighter aircraft spraying the road with machinegun fire.

Rumpel bounded off Erika's lap. Erika wiggled out of the sidecar, and Manny pulled her down into the ditch. The roar of the fighter plane's engines drowned out the spitting machineguns that kicked up dirt and rocks off the road. Then, in a whoosh, roar, and tremor, it was gone.

A Wermacht soldier said it was a British plane. It had sprayed the refugees because German Army units were camouflaging their retreat among the displaced people from Poland and the Baltics. Slowly, everyone got back on the road and continued westward, where rumors placed the liberating Allied armies.

Shortly, the motorcycle ran out of gas. Manny saw that the tank had been hit by something and there was a leak. After walking a few kilometers, Erika dashed off the road, across a field, and to the top of a rise, where she hopped and laughed and waved her arms. Smiling, she pointed down at the city of Dresden. Manny saw steeples and spires under a pale blue February haze.

"Dresden has not been touched by the war," she said. "It looks just like it did when I left."

They entered Dresden from the east and went directly to Erika's house near the heart of the old city.

Dresden was whole and unbroken—no signs of war anywhere. No bombed-out houses or fires or displaced citizens searching the rubble.

"The war has forgotten Dresden," Erika said. "Isn't it wonderful?"

Chapter 35

Manny stood back and watched Erika embrace her tearful mother while being overrun by the vision of his dead mother on the floor of the Kroner stable.

Erika's mother was worried that they had come home illegally. Manny showed her a letter from the Waffen SS captain saying that Manfred Kroner had fought "bravely for the Fatherland" and "should be decorated for valor."

Manny lied, "That letter means I received an automatic three-day leave."

"I did not think they issued leaves at this stage in the war," Erika's mother said.

"My whole BDM unit was killed by the Russians," Erika said. "Mutti, I think you should leave Dresden before the Russians get here. Go to Uncle Franz's house in Bavaria."

In her blueberry apron, Erika's mother, Marta, was a rosy woman. Flush cheeks, a silvery smile, rolled up sleeves, flour on her arms, dough in her fingernails, bread in the oven, chattering like a bird in the morning, brimming with the immutable hope of an iron-gray Prussian Lutheran. She didn't respond to Erika's warning.

After spending several hours with Erika's mother, Manny said he wanted to go to see his grandfather's house.

In the cool winter afternoon, Manny and Erika stopped at Grosser Garten Park Zoo. They sat on a bench in the park and ate the two small pieces of hard, dark chocolate Erika's mother had saved since 1939.

"When I was a young boy, my grandfather took me to this park," Manny said, remembering the Nazi youths who had cornered his grandfather.

"I feel so good now that my mutti knows I am well," Erika said.

Manny tried not to think about his own mother. He glanced at Erika Mueller's bright eyes and knew he had made the right decision to help her; killing Martin Ulricht and his father would have to wait. By now, the Russian Army had probably taken the town where the hospital was located. Most likely, by now, Hans Kroner and Martin Ulricht were Russian prisoners of war.

Erika hugged him in exhilaration. "I am so glad I met you. Are you sure you are only sixteen?"

"I just had my sixteenth birthday."

"I've never met a boy like you. You are very different from any of the boys I have ever known."

They ran through the park and down familiar streets. Each recalled people they had known, incidents and places they had experienced, hoping to discover something common in their childhood. They finally reached the street where Manny's grandfather lived.

"We grew up in the same city and never knew each other," she said.

"Dresden is a large city," he replied thinking about his cousin Menachem, who had walked with him down almost every street in Dresden, who had taught him how to play chess and to box. Maybe Menachem was still at his grandfather's house. If anyone could survive, Menachem would know how. Maybe all the Henkels would be there.

Suddenly teeming with hope, Manny ran up to the front of his grandfather's house and tried the door. It was locked. He knocked on it with a clenched fist.

Shortly, the door opened and a tall, blonde woman in a black dress stood looking down at him.

"I am looking for the Henkels," Manny said. "Are any of the Henkels here? Menachem? Any of them?"

"Henkels?" she said. "I don't know anyone by those names. This is the Schmidt household."

Manny looked around and past her into the entry foyer. "That little table was made by my grandfather in his furniture shop here in Dresden."

When she turned back to look, Rumpel darted past her. Manny ran in after him.

The astounded woman shouted, "What are you doing? You can't—I didn't—"

Manny darted around the living room, touching everything. "All these furnishings belonged to the Henkels. I grew up here. I sat on my grandfather's lap in that chair. There is the chess table where I played with my cousin, Menachem who lived next door. There is my mother's painting of this house. This was my home. These are the Henkel's things. Why are you living here? Do you know what happened to the Henkels?"

The woman was clearly shaken. She grabbed a stair baluster. "No. I don't know anything about any Henkels."

"I do," Manny declared. "The Henkels were Jews. Do you know what happens to all Jews?"

The woman shook her head coldly. "I have no idea."

"The Henkels were killed in a vernichtunslager."

"I don't know anything about political matters."

Manny picked up a glass-faced photograph of a man in a Nazi uniform with a death head insignia on his hat. "Is this your husband?"

"Yes."

"I see he's in the SS. I am in the SS. Our uniforms are the same. Ask him about those things you call political matters the next time he's home and needs a leave from killing."

"My husband is a respected officer in the Wermacht."

"He's in the SS. See that death head on his hat? That's an SS insignia. The SS are all killers. They kill Jews. I know all about high-ranking officers in the SS. I have seen a vernichtunslager run by the SS. I have seen the killing."

"Get out of my house."

Manny smashed the picture on the floor. "I don't respect bastards who acquire their homes by murdering the owners."

"Get out, get out!" the woman screamed. "We have murdered no one. I will call the Gestapo."

Two small boys came down the stairs and stood on either side of their mother on Aaron Henkel's blue and ruby Persian carpet, upon which was a ripped photograph of an SS officer and shards of broken glass.

Erika had been standing behind the woman, her face wracked, confounded. She ran around the woman, grabbed Manny by the hand, and pulled him out of the house.

They rushed down the steps and into the park. They raced until they were out of breath and fell down next to each other on the frozen ground while Rumpel circled them anxiously, nudging his nose into their faces.

Erika spoke first. "You're a Jew?"

"Yes."

"You don't look—"

"What did they teach you at that Hitler Youth School? Jews have long noses, wear rags, and their pockets are filled with gold?"

"Ja, ja."

"My mother was Jewish. My father is German. That makes me a Jew."

She didn't flounder. "I don't care what you are. I think you're wonderful, Manny. You got me back to my mutti, but I am so sorry your grandfather's house was taken over by that icy Schmidt woman."

"That woman knew damn well what happened to the Henkels."

Erika sat up. "What was that you said about a vernichtunslager?"

Manny sat up and faced her. "That's where I believe the Henkels were killed. In a death camp."

"Were they ill and dying? Did they have some fatal illness?"

"No. The Nazis take perfectly healthy Jewish men, women, and children there and kill them. The government calls them relocation camps. They relocate Jews from life to death."

"Where did you hear that? Why would they do that? I have never heard of such places."

"An SS officer told me about them. There are at least eighteen death camps. Thousands of Jews are exterminated every day only because they are Jews."

"No. I don't believe it."

"You had anti-Semitic lessons at school."

Erika nodded. "Ja, of course. Lots of words only."

"This is beyond words. I saw a death camp."

"Where?"

Manny told her about the camp, what the SS officer with the megaphone had said and about what Jacob had said and the short-lived uprising.

Erika hid her face in her palms, covering her eyes and shaking her head in disbelief.

"You don't believe me?" he said.

"I believe you, I can't imagine it or bear the thought of it."

"An SS friend of my father's said that they gas the Jews and then cremate them and spread the ashes on the fields of the Fatherland. He said Jews make good fertilizer."

She stared at him with incredulity.

He put his arm around her. "It's all true."

For long, silent minutes, they sat and stared at the elegant buildings, the leafless trees, and the gray February sky.

Erika wiped her eyes and said, "I don't want to be the kind of person who shuts their eyes or looks in the other direction. Tell me again. Tell me everything you saw at that camp, everything you know. I can't believe my country has done this."

"And they are very efficient in how they do it."

After he finished, they sat in silence for a long time. Erika curled up on the ground and stared at the sky. Manny looked up and saw a high-altitude plane flying silently toward the east. It circled the city and headed back west.

Shivering, Erika got to her feet. "This ground is so cold. We shouldn't be on it."

Manny got up, put his arm around her, and tried to stop her from shaking.

"I'll race you to that statue," she said.

As they ran, she said, "It's too bad you're so young."

"What do you mean?"

"You could be my fiancé, but you're inexperienced."

"You mean about women?"

"Yes."

"Do I look it?"

"You mean you're not? Did you meet one of the typical BDM girls?" she asked.

"No. She was a very experienced woman."

"A whore?"

"No. A beautiful lady."

"What's her name?"

"Helga."

Erika looked away. "So, how many times did you sleep with Helga?"

"I don't remember. I doubt that you have ever heard of the things she taught me. No, no, I'm joking. Once. Once only. Helga was a Christmas present. It's the only thing I've ever got from my father that I liked."

She stopped him. "Your father gave you a whore for Christmas?"

"Is that out of character for a Nazi?"

"Not in this day and age." She laughed. Her blue eyes glimmered in the limestone light of Dresden.

"Are you experienced?" Manny asked.

She nodded. "I hate the youth camps. They encourage us to become pregnant. The Nazis take the babies to be raised. Girls younger than I have had babies, only to be taken away and given to Nazi slave nursemaids. One of the girls told me they have all these women from the conquered lands nursing the babies in a factory nursery. The Nazis have all these big-breasted Polish women nursing German babies taken from their mothers by the Reich. It's wrong and very unnatural."

"Have you had a baby?"

"No, but I have had two arranged meetings, and I thank God that I did not become pregnant. I could never give my baby away." She smiled at him and leaned towards him and kissed him on the cheek. "I like you, Manny." She took his hand. "Come, I want to show you something."

Their run ended at the steps of a large, stone row house.

"This is my uncle's house. He's in the war. My mother takes care of it." She nudged a key out from one of the cracks in the stone.

Erika gave him a quick tour of the house. "My uncle is an antique dealer. These things are from all over Europe from different time periods. I think this room looks like Lucretia Borgia's poisoning parlor and the dining room looks like Emperor Franz Joseph's flatulating chamber. But the best room is on the second floor."

She led him up the mahogany stairway. In a room with a large, four-poster canopied bed, she said, "My uncle said that bed once belonged to Catherine the Great of Russia. My uncle bought the bed in St. Petersburg before the Russian Revolution. During the course of one typical evening in that very bed, Catherine the Great made love to a dozen Hussars."

Erika lay down on the bed and propped up a pillow next to her. "Come lie here with me. You can only see it from here." Her bright blue eyes beckoned, and Manny wondered if he correctly read their meaning.

When they were side by side, she said, "Look up."

The ceiling of the bed canopy was made of hexagonal mirror. "Catherine liked to watch herself and her Hussars."

They pretended they were making love. Erika was Catherine and Manny a Hussar. They rolled around and she laughed and said, "Next Hussar. Next. Number ten. Are you number ten? I like you the best. So far. But look at that line. There are so many more, and the night is long."

Their embraces and rolls and laughter and reflections became a holds that had no bounds. And shortly, they caught glimpses of reflections similar to those once seen by a Russian queen.

Chapter 36

Under the feathery scarlet quilt, Manny closed his eyes. He saw a jagged,

smoky land. Erika stirred next to him and said, "I hope there will never be

war in Dresden."

Upon opening his eyes, he was suddenly fearful. The possibility that the

sweetness of these last few moments with Erika would never be repeated,

rattled and shook his optimism. "It's all around us. Cities just like Dresden

have been bombed."

"I'm not going back to my BDM unit," she said.

"I'm certainly not going back to Werewolf."

"I'll hide in my house with my mutti. She will say I returned to my

BDM unit. No, that won't work. Mutti turns completely red when she tries

to tell even the smallest lie."

"Let's hide right here in this house. This place is perfect," Manny said.

"But tell your mother you're going back to the camp. We'll be here, we'll

be safe."

She sat up, looked around, and then regarded him with hope in her face.

"That's a wonderful idea. This house is very big, and there is a secret

hiding place behind a bookcase that only I know about. My uncle showed

it to me when I was little."

"And if you don't tell your mutti we are hiding here, she won't have to lie about your whereabouts to the Gestapo."

"Yes, yes." She sprang to her feet and hopped around the bed.

They got dressed and inspected the house and planned hiding places and escape routes.

As he put on the SS uniform, Manny said, "I hate wearing this, but I must to protect us."

On their way back to Erika's mother's house, they walked through the old Jewish section of the city. Manny said, "What happened to all the Jewish shops?"

Erika read the names on the storefronts. "Kraus, Brandauer."

While she intensely studied the faces of the people they passed, Manny mumbled, "German, German, German. Where are all the Jews that used to fill these streets?"

She stopped in front of a bakery. "This was Buttery Max's Bakery. I remember coming here."

"Now it's Erwin's House of Pork and Pumpernickel."

During the otherwise silent return to her mother's house, she said, "Suddenly, I don't very much like being a German."

Erika's mother had bicycled out to a farmer and purchased a small piece of pork, several potatoes, and a cabbage. She had also invited Minister Rudolph Kassel, a pale and creamy, thin-lipped, Dresden Lutheran. Erika's mother said that they were safe in Dresden because it was a city of mothers, small children, and old people. "Dresden has no military importance. It is not like the factory cities of Hamburg or Frankfurt or Hannover. I am sure they will not bomb us here in Dresden. We are all plain people." She talked about her husband, Friedrich, who had been killed in Poland in 1939 in the very first week of the war.

Erika asked, "Mutti, where are all the Jews of Dresden? All their shops have new names."

"Relocated," Kassel interjected. He wiped his mouth.

"To where?" Manny asked.

"To remote areas of the Third Reich," Kassel said as he cut off a slice of pork fat and slid it onto his tongue. "The reason for relocating the Jews goes back 400 years to what Martin Luther said. I quote, 'The Jews should be deprived of all their cash and jewels and silver and gold. Their synagogues or schools be set on fire, their houses be broken up and destroyed—and they be put under one roof, like the gypsies—in misery and captivity as they incessantly lament and complain to God about us.'"

He turned to Manny and said with great reverence, "I understand that you noble men of the SS are executing Luther's beliefs."

"Oh yes," Manny said. "The SS has their own interpretation of Luther's words. They are killing all the Jews."

"I don't believe that, Herr Kroner." Kassel smiled. "They are relocating them. That is the official policy of the Third Reich. That is the truth."

"Yes. You are right. That is the truth as told by the Third Reich. They are relocating them. From life to death."

"Now, now, Herr Kroner, you are surely hyperbolizing. We are a civilized nation. Germany is a nation of laws."

"You are correct again. There is a law that makes it illegal for Jews to be alive in Germany."

"I don't know about any of that Jewish business," Erika's mother said.

"But you had Jewish friends, mutti," Erika said. "For years we went to Max's Bakery. You called him Maxie and he called you Martie and he flirted with you. You liked him, mutti. I know you did."

"In the shops, yes, the tailor, the grocer, yes of course. They had the best shops. But I could never have a Jew sit at my dinner table because that is how your father wanted it. He never wanted one of them in his house because he thought they were dirty and sinful."

"Jews are cleansed from sin," Manny said.

"Jews think they are cleansed from sin through circumcision," Kassel said.

"Of course," Erika interjected. "I remember."

"You remember?" her mother said with raised eyebrows. "What do you remember?"

Erika stumbled with her words as Manny kicked her under the table. "I remember from the lessons at the Hitler youth camp. They showed us photographs. Jews are circumcised," she said. "That procedure is supposed to clean them of sin."

Shortly after dinner, Kassel left. Erika's mother escorted him to the door. Then she came back in the kitchen and told Erika she was very tired and wanted to go to sleep.

While laughing about the food that got stuck in the corners of Kassel's thin lips and the minister's blind faith in the Nazis, Manny and Erika washed the dishes.

Manny put his arms around Erika, "Maybe we should go back to the bed of the Russian queen."

Erika smiled and pushed him away.

Chapter 37

In the attic bedroom by 10:00 p.m., Manny could not sleep. He was making a mental list of the food they should get for Erika's uncle's house and how and where they would obtain it. He knew they would have to leave Rumpel with Erika's mother.

He was also thinking about Erika and Catherine the Great's bed. Her touch, feel and scent were strong and sweet and still with him. He went to the window and looked out over the dark, sleeping city. Rumpel moved around the room uneasily, something upsetting his animal senses. He'd come and stand by Manny's side, make an unfamiliar whining sound, then lie down and look up at him with his night eyes, full of knowing and understanding of a realm of discernment Manny could never comprehend.

He heard the stairs creak and saw Erika tiptoeing up. Rumpel never glanced in her direction, and only kept his eyes on the window. She came and stood by Manny's side and whispered, "I couldn't sleep. I was thinking about our hiding out. There is a problem."

He interrupted, "The food, right?"

"How did you know?"

"At night, we'll go out and steal. That's the only thing we can do."

"I'm not a thief," she said. "If I get caught, my mutti will be very hurt and angry and disappointed."

"You won't have to do it. I'll do it. I'll be what the Nazis expect a Jew is supposed to be—a thief and a crook. When we were walking back to your mother's house today, I was thinking about the provisions we would need. I saw a few stores that had possibilities. I wouldn't take much. There isn't much to take anyway. They wouldn't even miss the food, so there would be no calling the police."

"I can't let you do that."

"Many of those stores were once owned by Jews. The new German owners stole the entire store from the Jews. We're just stealing back what they stole. Or would you rather go back to BDM?" Manny asked.

"Never."

"Then it's decided."

"Yes." She smiled. "You are right. Those were Jewish stores stolen by Germans. It's justified theft as far as I'm concerned. I'll help you."

"There is another way," he said. "It's not risky at all. I could wear my SS uniform and buy the food. I would go to the front of any line."

"No," she said. "I would rather steal than see you in that uniform."

They made plans on the edge of the dark, sleeping city on the River Elbe. Suddenly, Rumpel's front paws were on the windowsill. His hair was raised as he barked at the night over Dresden. Manny saw an eerie, greenish light puff out somewhere over the big bend of the Elbe River.

"What's that?" Erika asked.

Manny opened the window and stared at the strange light. Rumpel's bark became hysterical, intense.

"I don't know," he said. "Stop it, boy, stop it. You're waking up the whole city." Rumpel wouldn't quit barking and howling. Manny held

Rumpel's mouth shut and turned to Erika. "Listen, listen. Airplanes. Hundreds of them."

He heard a deep rolling and thudding and saw lights flashing on the far edge of the city.

Suddenly, the black sky illuminated, and the city was drenched in a white brilliance.

Manny threw on his clothes. "Those are flare bombs. It's an air raid. Wake up your mother and get down in the basement right now. Run. Run like you never ran before. I'll be right behind you."

As Erika bolted down the stairs, Manny saw and heard bombs detonating at the far edge of the city. In a final glance through the window, he saw a wave of explosions rolling toward them, and heard the sound of many airplanes coming closer. Then he ran for the stairs.

Erika and her mother hurried down the stairs with the other occupants of the apartment building. Erika's mother said, "Why didn't the air raid sirens sound? Did anyone hear them?"

"I don't think they work," a woman holding a baby said.

Now the bombs exploded nearby, quaking the stone foundation walls, shaking dust down from the floor beams.

A retired professor from another apartment said, "Dresden doesn't even have air raid shelters. Nobody believed that Dresden would ever be attacked. That was very presumptuous on our part. Germany bombed Coventry and London. What did those unenlightened Nazis expect?"

"Be careful, Gunter, be careful what you say," the professor's wife said, looking around apprehensively.

"I don't care. The Nazis are ignorant because power is all that matters to them."

The common basement wall of the house next door had a man-size hole in it. Several women with small children were climbing through. Then a bomb exploded in front of one of the basement windows. The metal window frame flew across the cellar and hit a woman in the back and knocked her down. Then the lights went out and it was pitch black. Children and mothers cried and prayed out loud.

One woman said, "The whole upstairs is burning. We have to get out. Everything will collapse into the basement. We will be burned alive."

Erika's mother turned on a flashlight.

Manny and Erika went to the door that led out to the street. The main body of explosions had moved off, but there were straggler planes still dropping bombs.

Manny said, "I'm going to check outside." He opened the door. Smoke rushed through.

In the red fog, the street was all smoke, dust and sparks. Among the fallen, destroyed buildings, the dead and injured were everywhere. Erika's mother had wetted down some sheets and blankets and now wrapped Manny and Erika in them.

Erika's mother pushed everyone through the doorway. Manny insisted she go through, but she refused. "Wait for me across the street. There's a small safe spot there. See it? Go. Go." She rushed back down into the dark cellar.

Erika shouted and ran after her mother. "What are you doing, mutti? You can't go back in there. The whole house could collapse any moment."

Manny followed Erika back into the basement. In the darkness, they found Erika's mother trying to open a room with a metal door, saying, "The explosions must have jammed it."

Manny helped her pull it open.

Inside was a man holding a blanket across a small window. Sooty, broken glass lay on the floor around his feet. He was gasping and coughing.

They were all coughing in the steadily thickening smoke.

Erika exclaimed, "I know you! You are Max the Baker. What are you doing here?"

Max saw Manny in the SS uniform and looked to run.

Erika took Max's arm, "He's a Jew. He wears the uniform to help us. Don't be afraid of him."

Erika's mother rushed up to Max, took his other arm and the flashlight he was holding, and led him through the doorway.

As he passed Erika, Max said, "Your mother has been hiding me."

With the aid of the flashlight, they found their way back out to the street, where the air was slightly less smoke saturated, only barely breathable.

They ran down the center of the street, away from the fires and the collapsing buildings.

Manny and Rumpel were in the lead, followed by Erika, her mother, and Max the Baker.

It was difficult to stay together. When Manny felt Erika's hand pull away, he stopped. He saw Erika going back after her mother, who had retreated into the smoke. Max the Baker was nowhere in sight. Manny ran after Erika.

Then there was an explosion and a building collapsed. Its stone and brick facade crashed down on the street.

"My mutti, my mutti!" Erika screamed. "Oh my God. Oh, my poor mutti!"

The building facade had fallen on top of her. She had been crushed by tons of stone.

When the dust cleared, Manny saw Max, pallid and ashy, standing on the other side of the pile of debris.

Another explosion tore through the smoke and dust.

Manny grabbed the stunned Erika's hand and pulled her down the street. To their left and right were impassable fires. Rumpel ran into an opening between two buildings and they followed him through a shower of sparks, toppling debris, and stinging, asphyxiating smoke.

Finally, they located breathable air in a cemetery crowded with shocked and injured people. Erika fell to the ground and wept uncontrollably. A mother carried her dead child in her arms. A woman was screaming and shaking her fists at the bombers above the city, "Grossbritannien schweine!" British pigs!

Erika was inconsolable. "I have to go back. I have to find my mutti. She may only be hurt. There may be a space under that wall, and all we have to do is dig her out. We have to go back."

"As soon as the fires stop and there is breathable air, we'll return."

Several hours later, the fires and smoke had subsided. They ran back into the city. The dead were everywhere. Parts of bodies stuck up through the debris like broken branches. The devastation was vast, yet some buildings were intact. Streets were unrecognizable, the fire damage everywhere.

They found the collapsed wall and started digging. The air smelled of burning flesh. Their rib cages hurt from coughing. Their throats were raw. Their eyes stung. Erika was wearing one of her mother's overcoats. By dawn, they had dug out several bodies. The last one was Erika's mother.

Erika did not say anything, just laid her hand on her mother's forehead as if she were checking for a fever. She held her mother's hand in hers with care, as if she were only hurt. Erika's bright blue eyes were dead and lifeless as she looked down at her and chanted, "Mutti, mutti." Black, sooty tears streamed down her face as she looked up at Manny and scanned the others they had dug out. Manny felt Erika's wail was for everyone. Everyone there, in Dresden, in Germany, and everyone the war had taken suddenly and forever.

They laid her broken body on a blanket. Erika wrapped it around her mother, and they carried her to the cemetery. It was almost noon. Manny found a shovel in a bombed-out house. It was mid-February and there was frost in the ground, making the digging extremely difficult. By nightfall, they had buried her in a shallow grave. They laid a flat stone on the ground near her head, and Erika and Manny scratched her name into the stone with nails they had found in the ashes of a burned building.

As their rough engraving of "Maria Mueller" took shape, Manny said to Erika, "My mother was killed a few days ago. I saw it happen, just like you did."

She sat on the damp, cold soil, sobbing. "I can't go on without my mutti. I loved her so much."

Then he told her how his mother had been killed.

When he finished, she said, "You were no coward. You went back."

"When I find my father, I will kill him."

Holding back her tears, Erika said, "When I was a small girl, my best girlfriend stole my boyfriend. I told my mutti I wanted to kill that girl. My mutti gave me a mirror and said, 'Look at your face in the mirror when you say you want revenge. Do you like your expression, the look in your eyes?' My mutti said that. She was so wise. And now you see why she has died.

She hid and saved and died for Max the Baker. Did you see where he went? I want to find him. I want to ask him about my mother. I would never have guessed she was brave."

"She defied the whole Third Reich," Manny said. "She saved a Jew. That's how brave she was. We have to find Max. We have to help him, continue what your mother started."

"Yes, yes. We have to find him and carry on my mutti's work."

"We better do that now, before they come back and drop more bombs."

"They won't be back," Erika said. "There's nothing left to burn or bomb."

But that night, the air raid returned.

This time, the planes dropped incendiary bombs. The firestorm was sudden and intense. The fires sucked up all the oxygen, leaving very little air for the thousands of heaving, choking lungs of Dresden. The heat was intolerable. Erika and Manny were trying to get out, but the surrounding fires trapped them.

They threw a blanket over their backs and ran. The intense heat burned their hands and faces. Sparks flew into their eyes, and they could barely see or breathe. Air had been replaced by hot, choking smoke. They tried to get inside a cellar, but it was jammed with people right up to the opening.

Manny dragged Erika on through the firestorm. Rumpel guided them across bomb craters, fallen buildings, broken beams, jagged glass, dead bodies, and fires. Erika had fallen and cut her knees and palms. Manny kept pulling her ahead. They saw an opening down a small street and ran toward it. Rumpel turned away from his course and followed them. His hair was burned and his paws were cut.

The mouth of the street was choked off by a screaming mob. Manny turned in the opposite direction. He saw Rumpel bound through a thin wall of flames beyond which was an opening. Manny followed while clutching Erika's hand. They landed on hot ashes, scampered to their feet, and ran ahead. Rumpel ran to him and licked his hand. Manny could see out of one eye now; Erika couldn't see anything.

In the ashen clearing, they found some oxygen and an elephant that had escaped from the zoo. He was standing in place and breathing with great, laborious heaves. They continued on as more bombs fell behind them.

They were swallowed in a throng of humanity, nearly trampled, pulled apart, separated in the blinding, choking smoke.

Manny tried to stop, but was carried away by the swarm of people. He glanced back, but Erika was nowhere in sight. If she had fallen, he feared she would be trampled to death.

Against the flow of the shrieking mob, he somehow managed to fight back through. He searched for her among the hundreds of dead and dying. The planes were gone, but the city of Dresden was in flames, and Erika was lost in the smoke and fires.

His lungs and throat on fire, his eyes stinging slits, Manny continued his search as the pallid dawn arrived, a ruthless light exposing mass death.

Chapter 38

He and Rumpel searched for Erika all day, through another night and the entire next day. Manny went to the cemetery several times, left her a note written with black ash on a board, laid it near her mother's flat headstone, told her to wait for him there or write a note, name a place and time where they could meet.

He scoured the city's centers, where the displaced and injured had gathered. Erika's uncle's house was a heap of rubble. He found a shard of the Russian queen's mirror with melted edges and stuck it in his pocket.

He crossed the Grosser Garten Park, walking among the burned trees. In the middle of an unidentifiable street stood a house, the only house that had survived on the entire block. It was his grandfather Aaron Henkel's house, the house that Aaron Henkel had built with his own hands, the house that was now occupied by the Schmidt family.

He ran up the stone steps. The door was open. The house was filled with fallen plaster and broken glass, but its stone frame was intact. The fires had bypassed it. Most of the furnishings and carpeting had been removed. A man was carrying out a mattress.

"What happened to the woman who lived here?" Manny asked.

"Mrs. Schmidt made a big mistake. She didn't stay in the house. She and her children were killed running away. If she had stayed, she would be alive, and I wouldn't be taking her things."

"Those were not her things. They belonged to my grandfather. This was his house before the Schmidts stole it."

"May I take this mattress?" the man asked. "My wife is badly burned, I cannot get her to a hospital. She needs something comfortable to die on."

From the familiar window seat, Manny watched the man carry off the mattress, dodging rubble and broken glass. Directly across the street was the statue of Frederick the Great, who stood unruffled and oblivious to the destruction around him. Manny and Menachem had named every pigeon that shit on it.

The once-familiar view of his childhood was in ruins. Houses were burned and knocked down. Accustomed places looked alien. Where were all the usual faces and voices? He wanted to hear the bickering and laughing and crying of the Henkels. And his mother. He wanted to be with her for just one short moment more. In looking back at all that had transpired, everything seemed clipped and abridged. He could find no moment that lasted. Fires and bombs and the insane Nazis had annihilated all he had known.

He was tugged back into the darkness of the house. He sat down on the plaster debris covering the couch, where his mother had read to him when he was a boy. In a moment as still as death, within the cold shades and shadows that had once been fervor and light, he thought he heard the voices of the Henkels. Menachem muttering, "Checkmate." His grandfather asking, "Will you come for a walk with me?" His mother reminding him, "Put your scarf on, Ari." And his cousin Rachel perpetually cranking the Victrola to hear Paul Whiteman's American swing.

Then, in an instant of remembrance so acute that it could not be distinguished from reality, came a closeness with his mother that he hadn't even known when she was alive.

He woke and lifted his head from her embrace and she fussed with his tousled hair and smiled as she traced a finger on his cheek and told him that he had slept on her cameo broach and that the imprint of Aphrodite was marked on his cheek. He ran his fingers across the soft facial engraving and asked her if it was permanent. She told him that Aphrodite's imprint would disappear, but that he would forever be marked as a man who would always be surrounded by love. She held him and traced her finger across the fading imprint of the ruby goddess on his cheek. He asked her if she loved his father and why he wasn't with them. She said nothing for a long moment, then got up and shortly returned with a photograph.

"I keep it hidden in the attic floor. This is our secret. You must not tell anyone. Remember this man as your father, not the father who now wears an SS uniform."

Hours later, Manny awoke shivering in the rubble of the Henkel's house, thinking about his father standing over his dead mother in his black SS uniform.

He searched for a loose floorboard in the attic and eventually found an envelope. Inside was a photograph of his father as a student taken on the campus of Dresden University.

Downstairs, sitting on the windowsill, he looked at the picture in better light. This man, his father, her husband, had become a contemptible SS officer. How could his mother have ever loved him? How could she not have known what kind of man he really was? There must have been at least one telltale sign that he would become a mass murderer.

He walked outside and sat on the front stoop. Up the street, he saw a man laboring and stumbling, heading in his direction. The man froze when he saw Manny. He put up his hands in surrender. He was cut and bruised and disorientated and wearing a singed and burned fur coat. He threw up his hands probably because Manny was wearing an SS uniform.

The man's voice was shaky. "Just shoot me here and now."

For a moment, Manny thought the man was his grandfather Aaron. There was some vague likeness. Perhaps in the way he stood—tall, thin, and unsure on his skeletal legs. Then he recognized the man was Max the Baker, the Jew Erika's mother had hidden in her basement.

Manny seized the old man's spindly arm. "Come with me."

"Aren't your Erika Mueller's friend?" the man asked.

"Yes," Manny said. Up the street, he saw a band of men hurrying around a corner, looking around. One had a machinegun on a strap around his neck. Manny hauled the man into the Henkel house like a threadbare scarecrow. He ushered him into a corner of the living room. "Lie down over there."

First the man resisted, but then lay down.

"I'm not going to hurt you. This SS uniform is only a guise. I'm a Jew like you. Now, don't move and don't say a word."

Manny ripped off the window curtains. As he threw them on top of the man, he said, "Lie absolutely still." Then he scattered handfuls of plaster dust on the curtains and laid broken furniture on top of that.

He heard shouts and boots trampling down the street and up the steps. The Gestapo in civilian suits rushed into the room filled with plaster dust.

Manny was furiously digging through the pile of plaster in the middle of the room.

One of the men shouted, "Halt an, junger Soldat."

Manny coughed and spit and walked over. "Can't breathe in here."

He led the men outside to the front steps.

"Did you see a Jew pass by here?" one asked.

Manny brushed off his uniform, displaying the SS insignia and laughed. "I have seen no Jews. What do you think I have been doing for the past few years? Don't you know what my job is? If I had seen a Jew, you wouldn't be asking me if he had passed by me. Me? I am a non-commissioned officer in the Waffen SS. We are the scourge of the earth. The scourge of the Jews. You should be more careful with your questions."

"The Jews we're looking for were hidden by disloyal German families. The air raid and fires forced them out of their hiding places."

A very young fat man asked, "From your insignia, I see that you are serving in the Totenkopf Division of the Waffen SS. Have been in combat?"

"Of course," Manny said.

"Are you home on leave?" Another asked.

"Until tomorrow," Manny said. "I was looking through the house for something valuable I could trade for some schnapps to take back to the Russian front, but there is nothing but plaster and dust."

The Jew hunters trampled off.

A few minutes after the men left, Manny went back in the house and saw that Max was sitting up and coughing. After brushing himself off, he got up slowly and extended his hand for Manny to help him get to his feet. "My name is Max Steinhardt. What is your name?"

"Manfred Aaron Kroner."

"Aaron," Max repeated. "Aaron was the older brother of Moses, the first high priest of the Hebrews. You have a Teutonic first name—very odd, Manfred Aaron."

"My mother is Jewish, my father a German," Manny said, grabbing Max's arm. "Right now, we have to leave here fast. Very fast."

Chapter 39

On the fire-ravaged streets of Dresden, Manny and Max saw people carrying the dead to a nearby railroad station. On the platform and along the tracks, hundreds of bodies were laid out in a flea market of mangled and unidentifiable death, filling the air with the smell of burned flesh. People were inspecting the faces, looking for relatives and friends killed during the two nights of air raids.

Manny did not find Erika Mueller.

By morning, volunteers were stacking the dead in trucks like cordwood to be taken out of the city limits and to be buried in mass graves. More bodies arrived in a steady stream. A fireman said there were 50,000 dead.

Later, sitting on a park bench, Manny said to Max, "We need food. We have a better chance of finding food in the countryside. Let's get out of Dresden." He and Erika had also planned to make nighttime food runs out to the countryside, dig for potatoes, onions, and turnips.

In a bombed bakery, they found some stale and hard bread. They sat on the fallen boards that once had been shelves laden with buttery pastry and pregnant loaves.

As they walked out of Dresden, Manny resisted an impulse to look back. Other than Menachem, he didn't think he would ever see any of the Henkels again. He knew he would never see Erika Mueller and never his mother. Perhaps he didn't look back because he didn't want that wave of grief to overtake him. Or because he knew that his father and Ulricht were somewhere out in front of him, and he had to hasten to catch up with them. Perhaps that was why he walked so fast. That was why he believed he had survived and would continue to survive. His purpose was to avenge his mother and grandfather and try and live with the loss of Erika. That would be his life; that was all he had. Everything else was lost.

During the day, Manny and Max hid in barns and sheds of the countryside. Rumpel was their sentry when they slept. It was early on in their journey when Manny told Max about his mother's murder. Manny said, "When I find my father, I'm going to kill him."

"Maybe you gave your father a permanent limp," Max said. "He will always stand out for God as he hobbles to his judgment. That is much better than murder."

A few days before the end of the war near Gottingen, Manny and Max were sleeping in a barn. The barn door swung open and a group of armed militia rushed in. They pointed their guns at Max and Manny and shouted, "Outside, outside, now, now!"

"I am an SS trooper," Manny said. "We have the mumps—I think, maybe it's the measles. I hope it's not typhus or cholera or smallpox. It's catchy whatever it is. We made a couple of people really sick in the last town. I think they died. We're trying to stay away from people. We don't want to make others sick. Help us, leave us some food and water let us die in peace. Here, we can make only the rats and the pigeons sick."

The men backed away and ran off.

"That tactic is right out of the pages of *Huckleberry Finn*," Max said. "That's how Huckleberry saved the slave Jim."

Through the late winter nights, they journeyed westward toward the alleged Allied armies.

Chapter 40

In April 1945, Hitler committed suicide. In May 1945, three months after

Manny met Max Steinhardt, Germany surrendered. In 1942, Max

Steinhardt "the Baker" had evaded capture by the Gestapo; he had returned

late one evening to find his family had been taken away. He was one of the

last Jews left in Dresden. That night, he needed a sanctuary. The only

German he thought he could trust was Erika's mother, Maria Mueller, his

favorite customer at the bakery. When he appeared at her door late that

night, she ushered him in and knew why he was there. Maria Mueller hid

Max for almost three years. Her reward for hiding him was death by an

indiscriminate British bomb during the air raid of Dresden.

Benjamin was Max's grandson, who had been turned into ashes by the

death bellows of Auschwitz, along with all the other Steinhardts.

Menachem was Manny's cousin who Ulricht said had gotten away.

Menachem remained alive as Manny's new middle name and was

inspiration to survive. Under Max's insistence, Manfred Aaron Kroner

became Benjamin Menachem Steinhardt.

At an Allied displaced persons camp, Max and Ben settled into a room of a barracks that once held Russian prisoners of war. Carved and scratched on the walls were hundreds of names, of doomed prisoners. There were names of towns from Siberia to the Ukraine. There were personal notes to loved ones. The writers were all dead, and their wretched desperate messages were to be obliterated. Shortly after arrival, the refugees were given plaster and paint and the wall scrawls were filled and painted and the desperate and hopeless Russian messages were eradicated.

Max refused the paint. "With a stroke of the brush, I will not obliterate the memory of these men as quickly as the SS had with bullets. The walls in this room will stay as they are as long as I am here."

Max had contacts. Shortly, a reporter from a Soviet newspaper arrived and took detailed photographs of the walls and ceiling. A few months later, the camp moved Max and Ben to another room. Their old room was disassembled and taken to a war memorial in the Soviet Union. A Soviet official congratulated Max for refusing to paint the room.

While working in the kitchen at the nearby American military base, Ben learned English. By 1947, he spoke it well enough to become a translator for American Officers he accompanied on unofficial tours around Munich and excursions into Switzerland and Austria.

One of these officers, Captain Billy James, worked at U.S. Army Intelligence. Ben asked Captain James to find out what had happened to SS officers Hans Kroner and Martin Ulricht. Ben did not tell Captain James that his real name was Manfred Kroner or that Kroner was his father. He said that Kroner and Ulricht were war criminals responsible for the murders of Ben's Jewish family.

A few months later, the captain summoned him.

Billy James was a thick man with a bushy mustache and a corncob pipe. He was from Louisiana, and Ben had to listen carefully to understand the heavily accented English.

"Got some news, boy," James said, smoothing out the single sheet of paper on his desk. "This here's a report from our Russian friends. Says here SS Officers Hans Kroner and Martin Ulricht bought the ranch in a Russian POW camp back in June 1945."

"Bought what ranch?"

"They died. It's a back-home expression."

"How did they die?" Ben asked.

"Shot while trying to escape."

James slid the paper across the desk. "That there is the English version."

Ben read the report, thanked the captain, and walked out.

There were woods all around the refugee camp. That's where Max found Ben as the sun was going down. Ben had impaled the report about Kroner and Ulricht to a dead tree limb and was throwing rocks at it.

Max sat down on a stump and watched Ben for a while, then asked, "Why not just rip it up? You can't hit it from this distance."

"Kroner and Ulricht are dead," Ben said.

"Then justice has been done."

"I was cheated."

"Cheated? How?"

"I wanted to kill them."

Max walked over to the tree and retrieved the report with the hole in the center. "Read it to me."

"Why?"

"I want to hear it."

Ben read the report about the Soviet POW camp and the attempted escape in June 1945 that terminated in SS officers Kroner and Ulricht being shot.

Ben and Max sat down on a stump near the smooth, gray trunk of an imperial beech tree.

Ben crumpled up the report and threw it down.

"It's all over, Ben. They're dead. There is nothing you need to do. That is justice."

"That's not justice," Ben said. "Justice had to come from me."

"I wish there was something I could say about justice, but I am not a rabbi or a judge, only a baker. But I know this—you want revenge, not justice."

"For me, revenge would be justice. That's what drove me. I lived for killing them. Now what am I supposed to do? I don't know."

Max sat thinking for a while, then stood up. "From not knowing, all wise decisions are born."

Chapter 41

In the summer of 1949, Max and Ben were eating dinner at an outdoor restaurant in Munich when Ben spotted a man sitting at a nearby table who looked familiar.

When the man got up to leave, Ben followed him. The man soon realized he was being tailed. He confronted Ben and asked why he was following him.

"I know you from somewhere," Ben said.

"You, too, look familiar," the man said.

"Who are you?" Ben asked.

"I am Dieter Ernst Stample. And who are you?"

"Dieter? Hans Kroner's friend."

"I see now. I remember. You are Manfred, Kroner's son."

"Were you in the Soviet prison camp with him and Ulricht?"

"Soviet prison camp? No."

"In June 1945."

Dieter smiled. "In June 1945, your father was in an American prisoner of war camp not very far from here."

"How do you know that?"

"I was there. We were all captured by the Americans in April 1945. Ulricht, me, Erwin, your father. We had escaped from the Russian front through Hungary. We were in the Fatherland, near the Rhine, when the Americans got us. We were together in the camp about four or five days, then they separated us and interrogated me for many days. To save myself from a possible war crimes trial, I told them everything. The Americans were very interested in us because we did a lot of our dirty work in Russia. They wanted to know everything about the communists. I told them that your father was my superior and he knew a hell of a lot more than I did. They were very interested in Kroner and asked me more about him than about myself.

"I served about two years in prison. When I got out, I looked up my friend Erwin Klost. He had also served two years, but he had been with Kroner and Ulricht. He said that Kroner and Ulricht had been taken from the prison in September 1947. They were going to help the Americans with anticommunist tactics. He had spoken to Ulricht only briefly, and Ulricht had bragged how Hans was going to get them to America and that they were leaving that day. That's the last I heard. So, they were not in a Soviet prison camp, and they certainly weren't dead when Erwin spoke to Ulricht in 1947."

When Ben tried to contact Captain Billy James at the American military base to ask him about the Russian report that said Kroner and Ulricht had been shot while trying to escape from a Soviet prison camp, the American captain who replaced James said that James had been shipped back to the United States and they did not know anything about such a report.

Later that night, as they rested on their bunks, Max said, "I will never know the names of the killers of my family. However, you are in a better position because you know who killed yours. For you, there can be some sort of justice. Your killers can be apprehended and brought before a judge. It is good that they went to America. America is a just country."

"Just?" Ben said. "If they're so damn just, how come they took them to America? The Americans knew about SS killings. That report Captain James gave me said Kroner and Ulricht were in the SS. And another thing, that report was totally wrong. Kroner and Ulricht weren't killed. And Captain James is back in America and nobody knows anything about that report. What are we going to do?"

"We have only one option."

Chapter 42

On the *General Horace Greely*, a ship that during the war had ferried American troops to Europe, Ben stood at the bow, waiting for the daylight. He had risen before dawn.

The sun came up behind him as he focused on the horizon. Perhaps he would see her even before the land itself, rising above it as he had been told, that her torch emerged above a fog-shrouded horizon. After a while, he saw a thickening grey line where the sky met the water. Land. America. But there was nothing impending above it. No colossal statue.

As the ship approached the mouth of America, the Hudson River, he saw her. He knew what she would look like. In his pocket was a postcard of her given to him by an American soldier.

But he didn't have to refer to the postcard to know that her torch was held high, that her crown was a radiating circumference that she would be towering and beautiful, and her expression would be one of blind justice.

When he was close enough to almost reach out and touch her, he imagined that her torch, not the sun, had ignited the dawn. He stared at her eyes, and at first thought they were sad. Silently, he recited the words he had learned in the displaced persons camp from an American officer whose family had emigrated to America only twenty-five years earlier: "Give me your tired, your poor, your huddled masses...."

Those were not sad words. Her eyes were not rueful. Her expression and the words she was given by Emma Lazarus were magnanimous, human, and monumental. She was justice and freedom, and somewhere within her long reach were two killers.

He removed a handkerchief from his pocket and unwrapped the shard of mirror from the bed of Catherine the Great. He held the mirror so that Liberty's reflection was in it. A part of his own face momentarily eclipsed her, and he lost her briefly in the sky, where he saw the sad blue eyes of Erika Mueller.

The American Immigration officer on Ellis Island looked at his identity papers and said, "Benjamin, huh? Americans like to keep names short and quick. My name's Robert, but everyone calls me Bob. Welcome to the United States, Ben."

Chapter 43

Back in Kroner's living room, Ben saw that the electrified spark screen was bolted down through the floor and made of heavy, welded steel tubing and thick steel mesh. Impossible to topple or break through, too high to climb over without getting electrocuted. The gate in front was padlocked. He was imprisoned in a parlor, on a hearth fenced in by an electrified spark screen. Another sinister invention of Hans Kroner.

"Manfred doesn't want to share his Werewolf and Dresden adventures," Ulricht said. He dropped the bloody towel he had used to dab his nose onto the floor. "That's much better now. The bleeding has stopped."

Ulricht continued, "Before the war, your father was a chemistry teacher. I was a ditch digger. He had intellectual powers, and I had physical strength. He may have had more esteem in the higher circles, but I had the respect of the common workingman. Among the working classes, brute force is always more effective and popular than the intellect. The common man hates the intellectuals, thinks they're sissies and snobs.

"Martin Ulricht, the brute, the barbarian, the uneducated swine saved your educated father from death. Survival doesn't give a damn if you got a college degree. Without me, he would not have lived. Sissies die when animals run the world."

"And without me you would have been caught, tried, and executed," Kroner said.

"You're the one who returned to the Fatherland to find your Jewish wife. You did a very dangerous and reckless thing, my educated friend."

"You're an ignorant man, Martin. A man who has no appreciation of literature, art, or music."

"Hey, I'm pretty good with the American, Hans, a lot better with the slang, the language of the common man. So go pound salt, Hans the professor. How's that for some original American?"

"You're also a language butcher. You think you're so good with the English language. It's a joke. You can't even speak German properly. You kill everything you do."

Ulricht said, "We killed Yiddish, that's for sure. It's a dead language in Europe because of what we did, Hansie, my educated friend."

Ulricht laughed. "I am a toymaker. I am Santa Claus every year for a church pageant in Lake George Village. Hans and I are good and upstanding Lutherans. Sometimes, Hans reads the Bible from the pulpit, and I decorate the church at Yule time. What are you talking about? Toby Johanson is no killer. He has never harmed a human being. That was Martin Ulricht but Martin Ulricht has been out of commission for many years. And Martin Ulricht clearly recalls shooting a bunch of Henkels."

"Shooting?" Kroner exploded. "Shooting? What are you talking about? You took the Henkels to Switzerland. That's what you were ordered to do, and that's what you said you did."

"Shut up, Hans. Just shut your shocked, phony mouth. Did we find any Henkels after the war in Switzerland? No. We withdrew their money from your account. You personally moved the Henkels' money to your account.

You did that because you knew they were dead. So, what the hell did you think I did with the Henkels to make that possible?"

"You bastard," Kroner said, holding his head between his hands. "You horrible, murdering bastard."

"Don't lie, Hans. You confiscated their money because you showed the Swiss banker the phony last will and testament of Aaron Henkel, in which he transferred all of his money to you. Except for one, the Henkels are all dead. One got away on the road."

"Who got away?" Ben asked.

"The strong, young one."

Ben believed that the strong young one was Menachem. He tried to frame an image of what Menachem would be today. Most likely an Israeli military officer, possibly in the Mossad. He was a chess master at a very young age, and a crafty boxer who had taught Manny how to fight.

"You could never get enough killing. You were an addict," Kroner said. "Killing was your morphine."

"You are correct, Hans. I was addicted. Sadly, the supply of my addiction was cut off by the fall of the Reich."

Ben stood up.

"Get back down!" Ulricht shouted.

"Let him stretch his legs," Kroner said. "He can't get over the screen without getting electrocuted."

Ben saw that the screen came up to his chest. It would be impossible to vault it from a standing position without touching it.

Then abruptly, after Kroner had muttered something in German, Ulricht walked up to Kroner and pushed him down to the couch. "You get this straight, Hans. From here on, I will assume the position of directing our fates. You are through bungling. Like in baseball here in America. You failed as a relief pitcher. I am the closer. We still have a chance to extricate ourselves from this situation. I saved your life once, and I'll do it again. Do you read me, Houston?"

Kroner stiffened for a brief moment, then slumped and nodded.

"Say it, Hans."

"I understand you, Martin. I understand you perfectly."

"Good. Now, let's stop fooling around here and go get the food and let's eat. All this bullshit about the good old days has got me famished. I could eat an entire smoked pig."

Ulricht extended his hand to Kroner. "Let's shake on it, Hans."

Without hesitation, Kroner took the hand decisively and used it to pull himself up, then brushed his hand through his hair and walked toward the kitchen, saying, "You are right. You are absolutely right, Martin."

"You're spineless," Ben said. "You never could stand up to that son of a bitch. He was always in charge. You were and are an absolute coward."

Kroner didn't respond but continued on into the kitchen.

Ulricht laughed. "Continue, continue. Family feuds are so entertaining."

Ulricht occasionally dabbed a handkerchief against his broken nose. Ben could see through the large window that outside it was early evening, probably close to 8:00 p.m. He heard distant thunder. In an hour or two, it would be dark and most likely raining.

Kroner's voice came from the other room. "Are you sure you can eat with that bloody nose?"

"Of course, Hans. I hope you have some cold ones," Ulricht said. "I am hungry and thirsty from all this excrement—or is it excitement? I guess both apply."

"Are all the lights off?" Kroner asked.

"Yes, Hans. Everything is under control. And please don't arrange the food so neatly on the plate. Just bring it in. I hope the juice is on in our little fireplace prison. Is it, Hans?" Ulricht shouted.

"Yes. It's on."

"110?"

"Yes, 110," Kroner shouted back. He came in the room with a large plate of food.

"Aah yes, Hans. Very mouth-watering-looking. What did you get, Hans? I see Wesphalian ham, black forest ham, bloodwurst, Thuringer, pumpernickel, mustard, mayonaisse, tomatoes, pickles, and a six-pack of my favorite German beer. I won't have any problem making a pig of myself. That looks zo good, Hans. Don't fuss with it so much. It all gets chewed and vacated anyway."

"I had to drive sixty miles to our favorite German store to get this stuff," Kroner said, moving the slices of bloodwurst to the center of the plate.

"If I wasn't a wanted man, I'd go back to my old hometown of Heidelberg to get it." Ulricht laid a slice of bloodwurst on his fat tongue and poured a beer into a frosted glass as a drop of blood fell out of one nostril onto the slice of sausage. "Aah, there's nothing better than nice fat bloodwurst. Or this juniper smoked Westpahlian, or this fine teawurst. So much to choose from, so limited the space to put it. Houston, I have a big problem."

Hans picked up a slice of bread and set two slices of tomato on it. "Only the inside of a 747 is bigger than your stomach."

Ben saw a connector between the metal tile and the fire screen posts. He also knew he had to find a way to insulate himself from the metal hearth tile. The current would most likely go from the screen, through him, into the tile, and then back around again—like on an electric chair, his body was the conductor. As long as he didn't touch the screen, he was safe. Whatever he did would have to wait until it was dark. He'd go for Ulricht first. He had to knock Ulricht down fast, before Kroner could react. There had to be a weapon. He glanced around the room—food plate, forks, more knives, and his own sheathed filet knife on the coffee table, lamps, and beer bottles.

That's it—a beer bottle. He'd knock Ulricht out with a beer bottle. An unopened one.

Then, he glanced at the cobblestone fireplace. He could see that the stones were uneven, some protruded out from the face. About two feet above the hearth, on the cobblestone fireplace wall, one stone stuck out enough to place his foot on it. That stone would help him jump over the screen. He looked up at the vaulted ceiling and knew that his head would clear as he hurdled across.

"Too bad you can't have much of this food, Hansie," Ulricht said. "Your father has a weak heart, Manfred. He has to be a vegetarian. Just like the Fuehrer. Not me. I am a lion, a carnivore, and I love being a carnivore. Are you a vegetarian, Little Max? This black forest ham is zo very good with mayonaize. Would you like some? Perhaps your father will feed you, Manfred? Releasing you to dine with us would not be a good idea. Not just yet."

"What are you afraid of?" Ben asked.

Ulricht laughed. "A survivor of Werewolf and the Dresden firebombing demands respect."

"Would you like a sandwich or something to drink?" Kroner asked Ben.

"Would that make you feel better? Give me a last meal? Is that some Nazi tradition I didn't know about?"

"Manfred is such a wise guy," Ulricht said. He turned to Kroner. "I'm so glad you saw your error, Hans, and changed your attitude." Ulricht chugged the glass of pilsner and poured another bottle. "Manfred has not been a son for forty years, and he wasn't much of a son before that. You have your daughter Mandy and the grandchildren, all unmixed stock to the marrow. That is your family, Hans, not Manfred. Manfred's mother was a Jew. That makes Manfred a Jew. Manfred has been dead for more than thirty years; let's not resurrect him now."

Kroner walked over to the picture window and stood with his back to Ulricht, taking small sips from the glass of water and tiny bites from the sandwich.

Ben saw a long, thin black statue on a middle shelf of the bookcase next to the fireplace. It looked like it was made from a black stone; it was about a foot long and substantial. He could grab the statue by the head and smash its square base into Ulricht's head. The statue would be a more efficient weapon than a beer bottle.

Ulricht continued, "Nothing in history compares to the Final Solution. It was bigger than the Crucifixion. The Crucifixion was only one Jew. We did six million, Hansie. Tell me the power we had was not intoxicating. Wake me up. Was it a dream? Maybe the day will come again when we can be wonderful barbarians again. Right out in the open, Hans. Not in Germany, but right here in America. We can sanitize everything in these mountains of purple majesty, under these spacious skies of blue and have lebensraum and Judenrein from sea to shining sea.

"Right now, we have a big, big problem. There are many healthy witnesses in the Ukraine and in Israel who remember very clearly what SS Officers Hans Kroner and Martin Ulricht did. If we end up in Israel, the witnesses will come out like poops from a sewer pipe. Even our own Manfred will be a witness against us.

"I am positive that Manfred was heading straight for the Simon Wiesenthal Center to turn you in. That's why I interrupted your cozy reunion. I saw you needed help. Am I not right, Hans? You have always needed my help. If it hadn't been for me, you would not be alive today. Your father, Manfred, was lying in the hospital bed. One half of his leg had been amputated because of a blood infection caused by your swing of the ax. Horseshit had leaked into his blood, and the Russians were about to get us. I got him out of that hospital. I hid him and carried him and nursed him until we were safe."

Kroner stepped closer to the window glass.

Ben saw that soon it would be dark enough to grab the statuette and leap over the screen and kill Ulricht.

Ulricht said. "Tomorrow morning, when you wake up everything will be back to normal. And isn't it odd that Manfred, too, had changed his name? Benjamin Steinhardt. After the war, we looked all over Germany. All the refugee camps. No wonder we couldn't find Manfred Kroner.

That tiger is very, very smart, Hans. I'd want a son just like Manfred. I like you, Manfred. I respect your will to survive, your cunning character. You are quite the little cheater of the Grim Reaper. I think there is a lot of Hun in him, Hans."

In the dying light, Kroner muttered in German, "I wish there was another way."

Also in German, Ulricht replied, "Sorry, Hans. There simply isn't. Just look ahead and don't worry about a thing. Don't look back, my friend. You must never look back and yearn for your illegal Jewish family." Ulricht smiled and slipped another bloodwurst slice in his mouth.

Then Kroner switched to English. "I need a drink."

The thunder pealed and cracked, and the air was charged with burning voltage.

"Are you sure, Hans? Alcohol doesn't agree with you. But I'll imbibe with you if that would make it easier."

Kroner went over out to the kitchen and returned with a bottle of cognac and two tumblers.

As they clinked glasses, Ulricht laughed. "Nacht und Nebel. Hansie, my friend, it appears that Nacht und Nebel is fortuitously developing right outside the door."

Ben translated "Nacht und Nebel" to night and fog. Hitler's Night and Fog Decree had been implemented to make the enemies of the Nazi party disappear into the night and fog, into death by murder.

Ulricht slid over to the opposite end of the couch and with a full mouth exclaimed, "Hey, I have a good idea, Hans. Let's show Manfred our private little collection."

Kroner poured Ulricht another glass of cognac and said, "What are you talking about?"

"Okay, okay then, our big, big secret. Alle unkraut aus. All the weeds out. That little secret, when we were Himmler's personal gardeners."

"I don't know what you're talking about," Kroner said.

Ulricht dumped the cognac down his throat. "Don't play games, Hans. You know exactly what I'm talking about. I need some entertainment, and Manfred should know the whole truth and nothing but the truth."

Kroner walked over to the window, holding the glass down by his side. "I refuse to do that."

"Okay, Hans. I'll do it myself then." Ulricht got up.

"No, you won't." Kroner blocked Ulricht's attempt to reach the bookcase."

"Don't be a jerk, Hans. Get out of my way." Ulricht pushed Kroner aside.

Kroner ran in front of him again. "With your clumsy, alcoholic fingers, you'll blow this whole place up. I'll do it."

"That's the spirit, my old friend. You do it

Chapter 44

Kroner walked over to the bookcase, set his tumbler on the shelf next to the black statue, switched on a recessed ceiling spotlight, and removed six books, exposing a small door.

He extracted a key from his pocket, unlocked and opened the hidden door, and slid out a hard, black suitcase. He brought it over to the coffee table.

"Jews might call this briefcase the Ark of the Holocaust," Ulricht said. "Do you know what the Totenbuchs are, Manfred? Tell him what they are, Hans."

The heavy darkness of the thunder forged closer. Humid raven air weighed down the cabin.

Kroner kneeled by the open black suitcase and set two ledger-type books on the coffee table. "These two Totenbuchs are from Treblinka and Bergen-Belsen. Safely hidden are books from Sobibor, Mauthausen, Buchenwald, Sachsenhausen, Dachau, Auschwitz-Birkenau and others along with microfilm of official records that proves six million Jews were exterminated by the Nazi death machine. We have the original processing

numbers from each camp and the rest is on microfilm. We even have the
minutes of the Wannsee Conference that decided the Final Solution of the
Jewish Question. It belonged to an SS man who forgot to destroy his
copy."

Then Kroner stood up and walked over to the window.

Ben recalled Hannah Zar telling him that the Totenbuchs, except
sixteen pages of Mauthausen, had never been found because the Nazis had
destroyed them.

"Hans and I collected the Totenbuchs from all the camps," Ulricht said.
"The operation was called Weed the Garden. Reichsfuhrer Himmler
wanted to cover up the Final Solution. He was a chicken farmer, so the
chicken poops must have stuck to him. He wanted all the records and the
camps destroyed, especially the Totenbuchs."

"Himmler ordered us to burn all the records," Kroner said. "He was
trying to save himself, and wanted all evidence of the genocide erased."

Ulricht started laughing, "Remember the 1944 Christmas card we all
received from General Hopt. On the cover of the card was the number
2450 surrounded by a square frame of barbed wire. Inside, the card
displayed 2450 multiplied by 2450 showing a product of 6,002,500. That's
about how many Jews were killed by the Final Solution."

Ulricht stood up, walked over to the window, and put his arm around
Kroner's shoulder. He looked back at Ben and said, "Your father said that
the Totenbuchs are a record of an achievement never before attempted in
the history of mankind. What if someone in the future says it never
happened, he said. What if they say no one could have done this, no one
would attempt anything like the Final Solution? Your father was
foresighted, a visionary man. Hans insisted we save the books. Zo, we
didn't burn them. Hans defied that chicken farmer, Himmler. Over the war

years, we had collected a lot of Jewish jewelry, diamond, rubies, gold and such. We were very, very rich. Loaded, stinking rich. So, we paid off an American intelligence agent to get the books out of Germany and into America. This is an achievement that cannot be denied. Yet now, in 1978, some are saying the Holocaust never happened. We almost succeeded in exterminating the Jews of Europe; it happened, and we did it."

Ulricht gulped a breath of air and continued, "All of us, the educated and the uneducated, participated in the Final Solution. People like you moved all those Jews to the ovens. You moved them, and we removed them. Some of us good Germans knew about the killings and did nothing. That's how that went, Hansie the Holacauster. Do you think you intellectuals from the universities killed any differently than us common workingmen? Your paperwork, your shipments of masses of people ended up in our rifle sights and gas chambers. We were all one big family of Holocausters. We killed Jews because Jews were illegal."

"You enjoyed it because you hated Jews," Kroner interjected. "You, like everyone on this earth, are jealous of the Jews. You hate their money, their success, their influence."

Ulricht waved him off. "It is like a plague, you have to wipe it out. Jews were a plague, we had to wipe them out."

Ben said, "Let me see one of those books."

Kroner handed him the Sobibor Totenbuch.

Kroner walked over to the bookcase and stared. He wasn't focused. He moved some books around near the small door.

In the semi darkness, Ben leafed through the Sobibor book. There were dates and numbers and columns. Then he looked again at the protruding cobblestone and saw that it could be used as a foothold to vault over the screen. He didn't care whether 12 volts or 110 volts flowed through the screen. He'd take the shock.

Ulricht cut himself a piece of black forest layer cake. "What happened to the music, Hans? Play the William Tell Overture."

Ulricht smiled and said, "I know one big fact about you, Hans." He turned to Ben. "Your father's university education came in handy. Zyclon B gas was his idea. He suggested it to Himmler a few years before the Final Solution."

"I have to get some fresh air," Kroner said and walked out.

"Just the two of us now," Ulricht said, standing up. He stretched and rubbed his stomach. "All that bloodwurst and lager has my tummy in an uproar."

Abruptly, the door swung open and Kroner ran in. He was wet. "It's raining pretty hard."

"Do you have something for an upset stomach, Hans?" Ulricht asked.

"There's some antacid pills in the upstairs medicine cabinet," Kroner said. He sat down in the rocking chair.

Ulricht walked upstairs to the bathroom.

Kroner was sitting with his eyes closed, with his hands over his ears, sighing, making a peculiar sound, a lamenting echo in some private psychological madhouse.

Ulricht came back down the stairs and sat down on the end of the couch, closer to Ben. He leaned back and rested his head. After a few seconds of silence, Ulricht muttered, "Jesus, Hans, too much food. You should have told me to slow down. Let's go now, Hans. Let's get it over with."

"After the Ticonderoga passes by on its return trip. The storm is moving away," Kroner said. "It shouldn't be too long."

"I'll just rest a while," Ulricht said. "Don't forget to wake me up, Hansie. I wouldn't miss this for the world."

In the semi-darkness, Kroner stared out at the lake. Ulricht lolled his head on the back of the couch.

Ben's muscles tensed. He stood up. This was it. Right now.

With his left hand Ben grabbed the black statue from the bookcase next to the fireplace; he placed his right hand on the wood mantle shelf, his bare right foot stepped up to the fireplace's protruding cobblestone. In one swift spring he leapt over the screen, felt a jolt of electricity, jumped across the coffee table, and swung the stone statue at Ulricht's head.

Chapter 45

Just before the black statue struck, Ulricht snapped his head back and the square base swiped the side of his broken nose. Ulricht toppled to one side, squealing in pain, holding both hands over his face. Ben pulled out the gun stuck behind Ulricht's belt and aimed it at Kroner, who was staring in disbelief and stopped cold when Ben screamed, "Get down on the floor! On your stomach. Now. Hands behind your back so I can see them."

Kroner lay down on his stomach.

Ulricht's bloody fingers reached for the gun in Ben's hand. Ben whipped the barrel around and struck Ulricht on side of the head, knocking him out.

Ben yanked out a lamp cord, cut it off from the lamp with the filet knife that was on the coffee table, pulled Ulricht off the couch, and rolled him over on his stomach to the floor and tied his hands behind his back. Then, he cut another cord and tied Kroner's hands behind his back.

Ben picked up the telephone. As he dialed a number, he pointed at Ulricht. "I hope I didn't kill him. I want that bastard alive and standing before a Jewish judge in Israel."

"Bastards like Martin have more lives than a cat," Kroner said. "Only something more evil than Martin could kill Martin."

Ben spoke into the phone, "Hannah, it's Ben. I have SS officers Ulricht and Kroner up in Lake George. Upstate New York. Yes, it's definitely Ulricht and Kroner, and a big bonus. They have the Totenbuchs from many death camps. Yes, the real thing. A big cache of the Final Solution evidence.

"We're about 200 miles north of Manhattan. Bring your people. Take down this number and my friend Tommy Heno's phone number and address in Diamond Point. Once you get into Lake George Village, call him. He'll get you up here by boat. That's the easiest way. I'll call Tommy, and tell him that you're coming. Meet him at the Town of Hague public boat launch. He'll take you across by boat. Or bring some cash and pay somebody to take you across. It's a hard place to find by road. We're on the east side of the lake, across from Hague, New York. There is no street number. It's a dirt road. Everybody around here knows it as the old Hatfield's and McCoy's place. I'll have a bare bulb table lamp on in the middle of the picture window."

Ben hung up and dialed Tommy Heno's number and got the answering machine. "Tommy, this is Ben, it's an emergency. I'm over at a camp on the east shore, the Hatfield's and McCoy's place, three camps north of Shaky Mike's place. A woman named Hannah Zar will be calling you. I want you to bring her here by boat. This is very important, Tommy. Get back to me at this number."

Ben also called Dale's Diner in Hague to see if Tommy was there or next door drinking beer with Old Man Slapp. No luck. Tommy wasn't around, but the word was out. Ben couldn't call the police, because Kroner and Ulricht weren't on any police wanted criminal lists. As Hannah Zar had told him on numerous occasions, only Israeli agents knew how to handle Nazi war criminals.

Within five minutes, Ulricht had regained consciousness. The side of his head, his mouth, and his chin were bloody.

"Let's make a deal, Manfred," Ulricht said. He rolled over onto his back. "We have more money than you will make in a lifetime. We have nice, fat accounts all over the world. What do you say? Make a deal, Manfred?"

"I don't think there is much chance for that, Martin," Kroner said. "Manfred has his own game plan."

Stricken, Ulricht looked at Kroner. "We have to do something. Talk to your son, Hans. Talk to him."

Kroner did not reply.

Throughout the hours of waiting, Kroner said nothing while Ulricht talked almost ceaselessly. Then Kroner, lying facedown on the floor, asked Ben if he could use the bathroom.

"Endure," Ben said. "That's what millions of your Jewish victims had to do in the cattle cars going to the gas chambers."

Ben rang Tommy's number again and left another message. Two hours passed, but Tommy did not call.

Then the phone rang. It was Hannah. She had stopped on the New York Thruway for gas and called to see if everything was okay. Two hours after that, she called from Lake George Village. She hadn't been able to reach Tommy and was driving to the east shore camp. He gave her the directions.

More than an hour later, a car door slammed. Ben ran to the door and opened it. Hannah Zar entered cautiously. She glanced at Kroner first, then Ulricht. She walked up to them and looked at them closely, as if she were inspecting meat.

"You're alone?" Ben asked.

"The rest of the team is on the way from D.C. They're flying directly to the lake in a seaplane and shouldn't be far behind me." Hannah took out a cigarette and lit it as she walked closer to Ulricht and Kroner. Ulricht stared curiously at her, while Kroner just glanced up from the floor and then turned away.

"It's them. You got them." Then she spoke to Kroner. "The last time I saw you was in Hannover in '32. Manfred was a little boy. You and Sarah were so happy, so very anti-Hitler. What happened to you?"

"No different than what happened to you," Kroner mumbled. "We were all idealists when we were young. I became a National Socialist, you became a communist. I killed communists, you killed fascists. That's what happened to us."

"Where are the Totenbuchs?" Hannah asked. "I want to see them."

"In the bookcase, behind the *World Book*, there is a hidden cabinet," Ben said. "Inside is a suitcase."

Ben extracted a key from Kroner's pocket. As he handed it to Hannah, Kroner said, "It's booby trapped. If she turns the key the wrong way, the whole cabin will blow up."

Even the rain beating down on the metal roof seemed to stop.

"You're bluffing," Ben said.

"Go ahead and open it," Kroner said. "We'll all be blown into molecules. Personally, I would welcome that ending."

"Hans, you do it," Ulricht said.

"It's a touchy, sensitive mechanism," Kroner said. "You have to turn, push, and pull the key in a certain way to turn off the power. Very tricky."

"Do it," Ben said.

Kroner did not think about it very long. "All right. Cut me loose and hand me my cane."

As Ben kneeled down to cut Kroner's chord, Hannah drew her gun and pointed it at Kroner.

Ben got the heavy black cane and gave it to Kroner, who rose to his feet slowly and hobbled over to the bookcase. Then, without warning, he swung the cane around and jammed it into Hannah's stomach. There was a snap, and Hannah slumped to the floor.

Before Ben could react, Kroner jammed the cane into Ben's side. Snap. Snap. And Ben went down. Ben could see what was happening, but couldn't do anything about it. Powerless, he watched Kroner yank the guns out of Hannah's and his hands. He heard Ulricht exclaim, "Bravo, Hans. Bravo."

The sensation of being paralyzed was overwhelming. Ben couldn't move his arms or legs. He could see Kroner scurrying about.

Kroner untied Ulricht.

"Hans, my friend, you are full of surprises. You never told me that cane was a stun gun."

"It's not a stun gun. It's something quite different. A prototype. Scrambles up the nerves. No permanent physical or psychological damage"

"Nice work, Houston. Very nice."

Chapter 46

"Speed it up," Kroner ordered. "Get them both in the boat. Let's stick with Nacht unt Nebel, as we planned. If they start coming around, give them a quick shot. Hurry. Those Israeli agents will be here at any moment."

Kroner flipped some switches in the bookcase. From the hidden storage area behind the books, he removed the suitcase with the Totenbuchs. He also slid out a larger stainless steel case. From his desk, he selected a personal photo album. He placed the black case and the photo album in the stainless case and locked it shut.

Ulricht lifted Ben to his feet and dragged him through the door. As Ben started to regain some movement in his limbs, he tried to stand and break free from Ulricht but couldn't do it. He still felt paralyzed. Ben heard the phone ring as his heels bounced down the porch steps.

The strong wind and waves, the steady rain, lightning, and thunder had passed, and the lake was calm. The sky was overcast. No stars, no moon. Only a sporadic light along the far shoreline.

Lying on the floor of the *MANNY A.*, Ben watched helplessly as Ulricht dragged Hannah across the gunwale.

When the *MANNY A.* was halfway across the lake, Ulricht said, "Always just out of reach—that's us, Hans." Distant lightning flashed on Ulricht's bloody, white face.

The thunder cracked and Ulricht shuddered. Kroner gripped the wheel, and skewed his eyes into the black waters.

As Ben started to rise, Ulricht jolted him down with a shot from Kroner's cane.

Hannah had been completely knocked out and now, almost twenty minutes after the initial jolt, was regaining her senses.

Ulricht looked terrified at rising and falling black water. "Hans, you know I can't swim. Where are the life jackets?"

"I'll get one," Kroner shifted into neutral and crawled into the cuddy.

Ulricht muttered something in German, grabbed Hannah by the hair, pulled her semi-conscious body over to the gunwale, and heaved the top half of her body over the side, submerging her head under water for a few seconds.

Powerless, Ben watched as Ulricht pulled the gun out of his belt, turned Hannah around, and whipped the pistol across her face, while yelling, "Wake up you Jew bitch! Open your eyes and see what's coming!"

Ben saw Hannah's eyes open, saw the blood rush out of the gash on her cheek. Ben shouted, "No! Don't, don't!" But his words were extinguished by a thunder clap.

Then, swiftly, Ulricht pointed the gun at Hannah and pulled the trigger as Kroner crawled out of the cuddy with a life jacket.

Hannah's back was arched across the gunwale. Ulricht grabbed her around the legs, hauled, and shoved her overboard. "It's been a long time, Hansie. I'm a bit rusty, but that's one down."

"What the hell are you doing?" Kroner shouted as Hannah's legs slid across the bloody gunwale. "What are you doing? I had everything planned."

"You?" Ulricht laughed. "You had it planned? Don't make me laugh."

Ulricht turned to Ben. "You hurt me, Manfred."

Ben glanced at Ulricht. Their eyes met as Ulricht cupped his nose in his left hand and grimaced in pain. "You ruined my nose, Manfred."

Kroner returned to the wheel, shifted, and the *MANNY A.* moved forward.

Ulricht pounced on Ben. He punched Ben in the stomach, grabbed him by the hair and pushed his upper body over the gunwale. Just before Ben's head went into the water, there was a shot, and Ben felt Ulricht's grip release. Ben pulled himself back into the boat as Ulricht careened and slid into the transom on his back.

Kroner, pointing the pistol at Ulricht, screamed, "Not my son! You are not killing my son!"

Ulricht pitched around in agony. "You son of a bitch, Hans. You shot me, but you didn't kill me. When I shot all the other Henkels, I didn't miss. Right between the eyes. Even that Jew wife of yours, I got right in the heart. The SS Ancestral Research Unit was about to discover the truth about your Jewish wife. They would have shot you on the spot. I saved your ass, Hans, and for that I get a fucking bullet. My whole life has been for you."

Ben saw the beacon of a boat's spotlight in the distant darkness. He had regained movement in his arms and legs. He saw Kroner glaring at Ulricht.

Kroner walked back to the helm "We have come far enough, Martin." Kroner reached down and pulled up the pants covering the artificial leg. He flipped open a small panel just below the knee and removed a cigarette pack-sized plastic box with a metal watchband. Swiftly, he slid the band around his left wrist.

"What the hell is that? Another crazy electrical project?" Ulricht asked.

Ben heard the distant thud and clank of the approaching boat and knew it was a diesel. He suspected it was Tommy Heno's boat. He heard shouting coming from that direction. He also heard and saw the lights of a low-flying plane circling toward them.

Kroner switched off all the running lights. He patted his artificial leg. "This invention will bring us to Valhalla in an instant. I have enough plastic explosives inside my artificial leg and critically located throughout the boat to turn us all into ashes. All I have to do is push the button on this remote controller. It sends a radio signal to detonate all the explosives simultaneously."

"You fool, Hans."

Kroner adjusted the position of the remote controller.

Ulricht was lying on the deck, holding his shoulder where the bullet had entered. "Don't fool around with those buttons, Hans. There is so much to live for. We can still get away and stay together."

"For what purpose? Now it's my plan. Do you read me, Houston? Do you, you rabid son of a bitch? I have waited for this moment for a lifetime. Knowing that you're going to die makes me feel very, very good. More, now that I know you tried to kill my wife. And you failed. He failed, Manfred. She's alive. You missed, Martin. Mission failed, Houston. Failed, failed, failed. You're going to Jerusalem, you fat, ignorant son of a bitch. A Jew is going to put a rope around your neck and snap it."

"And yours as well. You're going down with me," Ulricht said.

Ben saw the searchlight moving closer. In a flash of reflected light, he saw the stainless steel case next to Kroner's leg.

A small seaplane was now circling to land.

Kroner extended the hand holding the remote switch. "You have about ten seconds to get off the boat, Manfred."

"Give me the Totenbuchs."

Kroner glanced down and moved his leg closer to the steel case. "Never."

As Ben slipped on the life vest, he felt a sharp blow across his knees. Ulricht had hit him with the boat hook, crawled across the deck and grabbed him around the legs. "You're not getting off, Manfred."

Kroner withdrew the gun from his belt, walked over to Ulricht, and shouted, "Let go of him!"

Ulricht clung tighter, tried to crawl up to Ben's waist.

Kroner's gun fired twice in succession and Ulricht released his hold on Ben's legs. There were two bullet holes in Ulricht's forehead and blood pooling beneath Ulricht's head. Kroner had killed him.

Then swiftly Kroner pushed Ben over the side into the lake and the *MANNY A.* slid away into the night.

The spotlight of the approaching boat swept over Ben. He heard Tommy Heno's familiar voice. "That you, Ben? We pulled a woman out of the water. She was shot, but I think she'll be okay. She said she's your friend."

Thank God, Ben thought. *Hannah is alive.*

Chapter 47

Tommy's boat headed south in pursuit of the *MANNY A*. Periodically,

Ben asked Tommy to turn off the engine. They listened, but only heard the splashing of the water against their hull. When the lightning flashed, they looked south, but did not see the *MANNY A*. They saw no running lights. They saw a seaplane land behind them and churn toward them. The *MANNY A*. must have been hidden by one of the numerous islands, Ben guessed. It was out there somewhere, but they couldn't see it. They continued searching.

The plane stopped near them and waved to pull up closer. Two Mossad agents grabbed the bow rail and clambered aboard Tommy's boat. Ben suspected they were Nazi hunters, Hannah's associates. The first man aboard asked, "Where is Hannah?"

"In the cuddy," Ben said. "She was shot, but not seriously. She'll be okay."

After the seaplane took off, Ben said to the Mossad agents, "The man who shot Hannah, Martin Ulricht, is dead. Kroner killed him. Kroner has a suitcase filled with Holocaust evidence, and he's out there somewhere. We have to get that suitcase. "

They started southward. About five minutes later, there was a detonation and a flash of yellow light.

Perhaps two or three miles south, a sundry of burning clumps fell into the water like a shower of meteors. Then, there was a reddish-orange glow for a minute, and then everything except Tommy's searchlight went pitch black.

When they got to the area of the explosion, there was floating debris scattered about. With a landing net, Ben started to scoop up the fragments.

One of the agents put on a life vest, dove into the water, and started picking up and inspecting the floating debris.

Ben shouted to the agent, "Look for a stainless steel or a black case. That's the Holocaust evidence."

Ben continued emptying the landing net on the deck. As he examined a small piece of flesh-colored plastic, he said, "I think this is a part of Kroner's artificial leg. That's where the bomb was."

The agent took it and smelled it. "Plastic explosives."

"Yeah," Ben said. "I suspect Kroner had it built into his prosthesis." He continued leaning over the gunwale with the net extended searching the black water illuminated by Tommy's spotlight, picking up every bit of flotsam, hoping to find a remnant of the Totenbuchs.

They found bits of human tissue. Probably the remains of Kroner and Ulricht, Ben assumed.

"Let's come back in the morning, Ben," Tommy said.

Ben shot Tommy a look and plunged the net into the water.

Tommy didn't ask again. They stayed until dawn and longer. Ben didn't find anything that looked like it was part of the Totenbuchs or the black suitcase he had seen on the coffee table. The stainless case was probably in pieces at the bottom of the lake.

That morning, they left.

As they headed north, away from the sight, Ben saw a New York State Police boat coming up from the south.

Ben took the police to Kroner's and Ulricht's cabins. Ben warned the troopers about booby traps and the possibility the entire house could blow up at any time.

Later in the morning, at the Glens Falls Hospital, Ben and Hannah explained everything they had seen and experienced to the state police and FBI agents.

Ben knew that Kroner had been a monster. Nothing could change that. Ben believed that even if Kroner had handed over the Totenbuchs, it wouldn't alter how he felt about him. There was nothing of any value that he could salvage of a hideous, cowardly father who had thoroughly and utterly destroyed himself and countless others.

But Kroner had killed Ulricht and saved Ben by pushing him off the boat. Did that final act give Kroner even an infinitesimal speck of redemption?

It did not.

Chapter 48

Strangling vines grew up the south and west walls of Baron Manfred

Kroner's stone mansion, their roots sucking at the moisture that collected

in the masonry fissures. Shutters were missing, windowpanes were

cracked, paint curled and peeled, overhangs had deteriorated. The roof of

the granite carriage house and stable had missing tiles, exposing

weathered, damaged boards. Thick brush and forty-year-old trees covered

what once were manicured lawns. The beds of variegated flowers were

now overgrown with weeds and nettles. The red currant bushes were lost in

the thickets. There was an old, but currently registered Volkswagen parked

in the driveway.

The Dresden telephone number Kroner had given Ben was now

disconnected. Ben had gone to Dresden with his reconciled wife Isabel, to

the address Kroner had given him, but had not found Freda. No one knew

where she and her roommate, another old woman, had moved. Ben tried to

find his grandfather Aaron's house, but failed. He told Isabel about the

night of the firebombing and Erika Mueller. Dresden was unfamiliar to

Ben. He remembered what it had looked like before February 25, 1945; this Dresden was different.

Ben and Isabel stood at the front door of the Kroner manor in the gray East German countryside. They waited, knocked again, but no one came to the door. "Abandoned," he said. He tried the door, but it was locked. As they walked around to the back of the house, he remembered running around the building after meeting Helga and her girlfriends. To his left were the woods where he had hidden Stork's motorcycle in 1944.

Behind the stable, on the edge of the old paddock area, was the Kroner burial plot. There, he found a knocked-over stone marker: Sarah Henkel 1909-1944. Tall grasses and wildflowers grew around his mother's gravestone. Kroner had lied. Ulricht had killed her.

Then, he walked towards the stable.

Inside the horse barn, he stared at the spot where his mother had died. The *MANNY A.* was gone. In the damp, cool, craven darkness, he writhed and wrenched with the memory of the single worst moment of his life.

He found a shovel and went out to the burial plot where Isabel waited. Carefully, he plunged the spade into the earth, dug a hole next to the gravestone, and planted the giant lily bulbs he had purchased in the nearby town. He smoothed out the dirt with his hands, stood up, and said a silent prayer—jumbled words, confusing rubble he tried to put together into something that made sense. But in the end, the only words that came were, "I'm sorry I failed you."

Isabel took his hand and led him away. As they were opening the car doors, an old woman opened the carved oak front door.

"Can I help you?"

Ben went back up the cracked marble walk and asked, "Does Freda Kroner live here?"

"Yes, I am Freda Kroner. Who are you?"

"Freda? It's you? I am Manfred Kroner, Manny."

"Manfred? I can't believe it. My God, my God. It can't be. I thought you were dead. Come here, come here."

As Freda hugged him, not holding back her tears, she said, "Luckily, I looked out of the window and saw the strange car and two people I did not know. I cannot hear so good anymore. We get no visitors anyway. Mein Gott, Manfred, mein Gott, it is you. This is such a wonderful day."

"This is my wife, Isabel."

In the parlor, another old woman, wrapped in an embroidered shawl, sat near a window. She held a teacup between both hands, as if to warm them.

The old woman stared at Ben.

Tears began to well in her eyes, her hands started to shake, and the teacup fell and broke on the floor.

"Ari...?"

The sound of her voice jarred him. Slowly, he moved closer to her. He felt like an apparition floating through memories. She looked fragile, like the thin, broken teacup on the floor. Through the tottering air, she said, "Ari." Her hands were clasped tightly, blood reddening her fingertips. The stupor in her eyes transformed into the shock of a sudden awakening. He saw them luster, saw the emptiness in them dissolve.

She tried to get up, but fell back in the chair. Ben got down on his knees next to the chair and took her thin hand. Her free hand floated up and smoothed his hair. He thought he detected the faint trace of lilly of the valley.

She sighed deep and long. It came at once, and then together with him, a rueful sob, like a wind outside a stone wall, a lament, a sigh, a bittersweet release with his mother whispering, "Ari, Ari."

Chapter 49

Several weeks later, Ben received a letter and no return address. It was postmarked Cairo, Egypt.

Dear Manfred,

I could not envision being hauled off to Israel in blindfolds or handcuffs or disguises or the back of my hand covering my face in shame. Getting snatched off like Eichmann is not how I visualized my final days. It struck a chord when you said Martin did not have the guts to turn himself into Jewish authorities and stand trial for his crimes. At that moment, I realized what I had to do, and knew I had the courage to do it.

After I left you in the night waters of Lake George, and I was far enough away, I removed the artificial leg with the rigged explosives and put on one I had designed for swimming with detachable flappers. Then, I swam to shore with all the evidence of the Holocaust safely in a floating waterproof container. When I was standing on land, I blew up the *MANNY A.* with a remote radio control.

I had a small camp on the west side of the lake under another name. I also kept a car there, equipped with everything I needed to get away. That's how I escaped.

Now I am in Cairo, sitting on a bench, watching the Nile flow to the sea and preparing to cross the Suez and Sinai. As Moses did to free the Jews, I will free myself by bringing to the Jewish people undeniable evidence of the Final Solution. The end of my journey will be Israel. I hope that what I do will change your view of me in some small way. I have been a monster. I cannot go back to the past and change it, but I can change that the Holocaust is never doubted.

As soon as I arrive in Israel, I will turn myself into police officials to stand trial for crimes against the Jewish people. I will provide their prosecutors with the evidence to convict me. The films and the Totenbuchs that I took with me from the *MANNY A.* are now safely hidden in the United States. As soon as I arrive in Israel, I will inform Jewish authorities as to their location. If, for some unseen reason or circumstance, it becomes necessary for me to reveal to you the exact location of the Totenbuchs, I will do so. It is too dangerous for you to know this information now. I have recently learned that when we were living in Argentina, a drunken Martin Ulricht had bragged to another SS man that Hans Kroner possessed all the Final Solution records, and that Himmler's order to destroy them had been disobeyed. I fear I have to get the Totenbuchs to Israel before the neo-Nazis or those ex SS men catch up with me.

I paid American Army Intelligence officer Billy James a lot of money to bring the Totenbuchs to the United States after the war. For more money he gave them back to me when we arrived in the United Sates. Money kept him silent. But then, to gain his absolute silence, Martin killed him.

Neo-Nazis and other anti-Semitic movements, in their attempts to deny the Holocaust, do not want this evidence made public. Their mission is to propagate the lie that the Holocaust was a hoax. It wasn't. It happened. I saw it, I did it. The numbers are accurate. The Nazi death machine murdered six million Jews.

My punishment has to be the sentence of death. It has to be carried out by the people I attempted to erase from the face of the earth.

I hope that my evidence and testimony will stop this revisionist cabal that is attempting to deny the Holocaust. The Totenbuchs and films prove it beyond a doubt. I was involved in Himmler's operation "Weed the Garden," the mission carried out by me to destroy Nazi records of the Final Solution. The destruction of those records never happened. I saved them.

When I read about the reunion with your mother in a newspaper, I was elated. At least now I know that you did not lose everything. I am glad that she visited you in America and that you took her to Hollywood. She loved American film actors, especially Clark Gable.

Please contact my sister Freda and tell her what I am doing.

Soon, you will read about me in the newspapers. As surely as the water at the source of the Nile ends up in the sea, my journey will terminate in Israel. That is where I am going. I am guilty. I am a coconspirator and co-criminal of the Holocaust. I am taking responsibility, however small, and I go fearlessly towards it.

Your father,
Hans Kroner

Chapter 50

One year after Ben received the letter from his father, there still was no news about Hans Kroner surrendering to Israeli authorities. Immediately after receiving the letter, Ben had contacted Hannah Zar and had given it to her.

Israeli agents had scoured Cairo and other Mideast cities. Kroner had not been found.

Among Nazi hunters, there was renewed enthusiasm about finding Kroner and all the Holocaust evidence he possessed. Hannah Zar, recovered from Ulricht's gunshot, searched for Kroner and the Totenbuchs with renewed fervor. Hannah believed the Totenbuchs were somewhere in the United States. Ben had suggested to Hannah that the Totenbuchs could be somewhere on the bottom of Lake George in a waterproof container built by Kroner, most likely in the area where he had blown up the *MANNY A.* Several months of renewed underwater search in that area by an Israeli team had not been successful. The camp on the west side of Lake George from which Kroner had escaped, and the two camps on the east side of the lake and the surrounding grounds, were thoroughly searched. The Totenbuchs were not found.

Five years later, neither Kroner, nor Final Solution records, had surfaced.

But the hunt went on for the evidence by factions who wanted it revealed, and by factions who wanted it destroyed.

Ben had seen Kroner's voluminous official Nazi proof of the magnitude of the Holocaust. There were Totenbuchs from all the death camps showing the numbers of Jews killed at each camp, official papers from the January 1942 Wannsee Conference where the Final Solution was decided, microfilm of countless SS orders regarding shipments of Jews to specific camps and shipment orders signed by Adolph Eichman and other directives authorized by high ranking Nazi officials.

Volumes of official Nazi records of the Final Solution were out there somewhere. The records had existed and still exist.

That was beyond denial.

ACKNOWLEDGEMENTS

This book could not have been possible without the support and help of my children: Lisa, Kristen, and Jeremiah. Also, I want to thank my greatest story audience, my grandchildren: Sam, Cassie, Kyla, and Colette.

To my extended family and friends who offered advice, criticism and encouragement, I thank you. I am especially grateful to Don MacDougall who carefully read the manuscript more than once and offered insightful observations. And Lisa Rae Vancans who worked diligently and never hesitated to help me with the computer challenges I faced.

I want to thank all participants, friends and strangers, for their votes during the Kindle program.

Editing by Lisa Cerasoli and her group was uplifting and on the mark.

The cover by Keli Maffei powerfully captured the theme of the story.

Always, my greatest thanks goes to my wife Norine for her many manuscript readings and ongoing discussions. Her abiding support, encouragement and Italian cooking sustained me to finish this book.

Thank you all.

Made in the USA
Las Vegas, NV
13 June 2023